AMIAYA ENTERTAINMENT
PRESENTS

Flower's Bed

A NOVEL
BY
ANTOINE "INCH" THOMAS

This book is a work of fiction.

Names, characters, places and incidents are either a product of the Author's imagination or are used fictitiously and any resemblance to actual persons, living or dead, events, or locales is entirely coincidental.

If you purchase this book without a cover, you should be aware that this book may have been stolen property and reported as "unsold and destroyed" to the publisher. In such case neither the author nor the publisher has received any payment for this "stripped book."

Written by Antoine Thomas for

Amiaya Entertainment

Published by ATAE, Inc.

Cover Design by Apollo Pixel

&

Amiaya Entertainment,

Printed in the Canada

ISBN: 0-9745075-0-4

[1. urban — fiction. 2. Drama —Fiction. 3. Bronx — Fiction]

This book was written in F.P.C. Lewisburg 2002

DEDICATION

This book is dedicated to my lovely wife, Tania, and my precious little princess Amiaya. My mother, Sonja, and my sisters, Danita and Melissa.

Also, my nieces, Tiarra and Tatiana, my aunts and all of my female cousins. I dedicate this to all of you for being Black, and staying strong.

Peace!

by Antoine "Inch" Thomas

PROLOGUE...

Long before the arrival of the European Caucasian, the patch of land now called The Bronx was treasured by the spirited Indian people. Black Americans and Latinos would go on to blossom there, and by the early 1930s, the African American and Hispanic population had grown considerably, and some became business owners. Between 1930 and 1950, the stretch of busy bodega shops on the Grand Concourse fed the local economy considerably. After the second world war, however, the money the Bronx brought in began to dry up. The Italian store owners that lined both sides of the Grand Concourse left their tiny living quarters for lavish homes on Long Island. By the 1960s, most businesses would lose out to the new businesses that erupted on Fordham and Boston Roads as well as Third Avenue. Thereafter, people from the West Indies, Santo Domingo and Nigeria would become a part of its flourishing population. By the 80s and 90s, crack cocaine flooded the borough with destruction.

In the Claremont section of the Bronx, Ms. Melinda Abrams, her husband, Raymond, and their daughter, Flower, struggled to survive as the city's deficit kept the poor impoverished and indigent while its so-called laws kept the rich wealthy.

CHAPTER ONE

Summer of 1989 ...

"Mom! Mom! Mom! Hurry up! We're going to be late!" said nine-year-old Flower, jumping up and down with excitement. At her Bronx apartment in Claremont Projects she was clad in a bright yellow flower printed summer dress.

"Girl, you better wait a damn minute! I have to get my keys!" replied Mrs. Melinda. Mrs. Melinda, Flower's mother, was dressed in beige cotton shorts and a white T-shirt with the "Just Say No" slogan printed on the front of it.

Mrs. Melinda grabbed the keys to her Nissan Maxima and met her excited daughter by the elevator.

In her animated state, Flower continued, "Mommy, everybody's going to be there! I invited all of my friends from school, and all of my friends from around here." Flower was so excited that she wouldn't stop jumping around.

"Girl, I'm walking you into that skating rink and once I know that you're safe and that your cake has arrived, I'm off to work," said Mrs.

Melinda locking her apartment door.

"Is Daddy going to be there?" asked Flower with her most precious little smile as she anxiously danced around her mom in circles.

"Of course your father's going to be there honey. He never misses any of your birthday parties," said Mrs. Melinda softly pinching her daughter's cheek and gently wiggling Flower's head back and forth.

When the elevator door opened, Mrs. Melinda and her daughter entered and rode the seven floors down to the lobby. When the door opened, Flower saw her best friend, Rosalyn.

"Ros! Ros!" yelled Flower excitedly, running to the open arms of her best friend and receiving a warm hug.

"Hiii!" replied Rosalyn, Flower's ten-year-old best friend, who also happens to live one floor above Flower on the eighth floor.

"Is your mom taking me along with y'all?" she asked.

"Yes I am," said Mrs. Melinda, answering Rosalyn's question as they exit the building. Outside, Mrs. Melinda hit the alarm on her double parked Nissan unlocking its doors. The two children anxiously hopped up into the back seat and buckled up while Mrs. Melinda did the same in the driver's seat.

The 20-minute drive from Mrs. Melinda's home on 169th Street and Washington Avenue to the Skate Key skating rink on White Plains Road and Allerton Avenue, also located in the Bronx, seemed like it flew by in no time at all due to the fact that Flower and Rosalyn were having the time of their lives chatting about how much fun they were going to have at Flower's ninth birthday party. Finally arriving, Mrs. Melinda double parked her Nissan directly at the Skate Key's front door and exited the vehicle with the two excited girls.

"Excuse me sir," said Mrs. Melinda to the Skate Key security guard who was standing at the entrance door searching skaters for weapons.

"Yes ma'am, are you invited to the birthday party?" asked the humongous dark-skinned bouncer responding to Flower's mother with a question.

"Not really, but my daughter is the birthday girl," she said with a touch of sarcasm.

"Oh, I'm sorry. You must be Mrs. Melinda Abrams," said the bouncer, apologizing for his mistake. "And this must be the birthday girl," he added, not knowing which girl was Flower.

"It's my birthday Mister! I'm nine years old now," said Flower to the bouncer. She was in her bunny hop mode again.

"You are? Happy birthday young lady!" said the bouncer kneeling down making himself the same height as Flower.

Smiling, Flower bashfully rocked side to side and said, "Thank you."

"Well then, you guys go right on in."

"Go on girls. And give mommy her kiss," said Mrs. Melinda as Rosalyn and Flower ran back to her to give her both a hug and a kiss. "Y'all better behave in there too. And have fun kids. I love you!" added Mrs. Melinda.

"I love you too Mommy," said Flower as she and Rosalyn dashed into the Skate Key joining the other children who were entertaining themselves in group games.

"Excuse me sir, my husband is on his way. He'll supervise. His name is Raymond, okay? Also, here's my number if there are any problems," said Flower's mom passing the bouncer her number on a ripped piece of paper bag. "I have to leave for work now, but my husband will make sure that the party runs smoothly." Mrs. Melinda was pushed for time. She turned and headed back to her vehicle.

Before she reached her car, she turned back around and asked, "Has her cake arrived yet?"

"The catering people just called before you pulled up Mrs. Abrams. They told us that the cake is on its way," said the bouncer.

Standing halfway in her car, Mrs. Melinda said, "Okay, thank you." She waved goodbye to the guy then slowly drove off.

The party started at 7 p.m. and ended shortly after 10:30. All the kids had a great time. Flower pinned the tail on the donkey, she bobbed the most apples, and she ate the biggest piece of cake. After having a fun-filled evening, everyone cleared out from the skating rink. Raymond, Flower and Rosalyn made their way back home in Raymond's Alfa Romeo Milano. They walked Rosalyn home and walked one flight down the stairs to their own apartment. After locking the door behind them, Raymond rushed to the bathroom, then he went into Flower's room leaving Flower glued to the television set that is always left on when they leave the house.

"Flower! Flower!" yelled Raymond.

"Yes Daddy." Flower barely moved. Her animated video tape had put her into a momentary trance.

"Come here. Come to Daddy."

"Okay. Where are you Daddy?" asked Flower running into her mother and father's bedroom.

"I'm in your room Flower."

"Yea! Yea! Daddy's gonna tuck me in!" she exclaimed. Flower got to her room and noticed Raymond in her bed underneath the covers.

Flower placed her hands at her hips and said, "What are you doing Daddy? You know you're too big to be in my bed."

"Yeah, I know, but Daddy loves Flower's bed. Now come here and get under the covers with Daddy.” Raymond was tapping the bed encouraging Flower to come lay beside him.

Flower sensed something was very strange. “Daddy,” she said, dropping her hands from her waist.

“Come on,” said Raymond waving her to come closer to him.

“Okay,” said Flower. Unmindful, she got into the bed with her father.

“Flower, you know you can’t come in here with your dress on. Take it off and put it in the chair.”

“Okay Daddy,” said Flower, getting undressed and covering her tiny chest while jumping back into her bed where her father lay scheming.

“Daddy,” said Flower innocently.

“Huh.”

“Are you going to read to me?” she asked. Flower was a princess, but Raymond didn’t care.

He replied, “No honey, Daddy has something special for you tonight that’s better than reading.”

“Better than reading!” said Flower excitedly. “What is it? Is it a new doll baby?” asked Flower covering her eyes with her hands hoping to be surprised with a toy.

“Nope, I have something better, but you have to promise me that you won’t tell Mommy, okay? You promise?” he said looking at her.

“Yes Daddy. I promise. I cross my heart and hope to die that I won’t tell.”

Just then, Raymond flung the covers off of himself revealing his swollen manhood.

“Daddy,” screamed Flower.

“What baby? This is your present. But you can’t tell Mommy like I said."

"Daddy, I don't want your pee pee. I'm scared Daddy! You're scaring me," she cried.

Raymond snapped. He pointed his index finger at her and raised his voice. "Flower, put your damn mouth around it or I will tell Mommy that you touched me. Who do you think she is going to believe huh? You, or me? Who?"

"Daddy," she said crying now. "Stop. Stop it please."

"Do you want Daddy to hurt you? 'Cause I will. I'll hurt you. You and Mommy," he continued.

"No Daddy. No. Don't hurt us. Please. Why are you mad at me? What did I do?" asked Flower, confused and not knowing what it was that made her father act like this towards her. She tried to cover up.

"Shut up stupid! You're stupid! Shut the hell up! Now put your mouth on it or I'm going to hurt you! I'll hurt Mommy too! Do you hear me?"

Flower had no choice but to comply, and for the next 45 minutes, Raymond sexually assaulted poor little Flower. She cried and cried begging him to stop, but he wouldn't. He just continued having his way with her until he was done. At one point, Flower almost blacked out from the intense pain. All she kept hearing was, "I'll hurt you! You and Mommy!, over and over again.

When Raymond finished up, he took a bath with Flower and showed her how to wash up real good. He even held her head up under the water for ten seconds at one point, scaring her half to death. Afterwards, he tucked her in her bed and waited for his wife Melinda to come home.

Six years later ...

"No Daddy! No Daddy! Noooo!" screamed Flower awakening

herself and sitting up as her mother ran into her bedroom noticing the beads of sweat all over Flower's face.

"Flower, are you okay sweetheart?" asked Mrs. Melinda who positioned herself on the bed beside her terrified daughter.

"It was just another nightmare darling," she added as she comforted 15-year-old Flower by caressing and embracing her tightly in her arms.

"I'm okay Mommy. I'm fine. Just get me something to drink, please," said Flower rubbing her teary eyes.

"Sure honey, I'll be right back," said Mrs. Melinda as she retrieved Flower a glass of water from the kitchen. She returned a few moments later, sat beside Flower and handed the water to her.

"Flower, how are you, really?" Mrs. Melinda was concerned.

"I'm okay, Mommy. It was just another bad dream. I'll be fine," said Flower cracking a tiny smile.

"I know honey. But sometimes you have to talk to someone. So remember that I'm always here for you. I'll be here no matter what. But I strongly suggest that you at least give Mrs. Berkowitz an opportunity to sit down and talk with you darling."

"Mom! I don't need to talk to anybody's psychiatrist. I'm not crazy." Flower raised her head and shook the hair from her face.

Helping her brush the hair from her face, Mrs. Melinda said, "She's not a psychiatrist dear, she's the family counselor and I know you're not crazy. But when Raymond died, it affected the both of us. I just decided to get a little help dealing with it, that's all. Honey, there are so many families that experience tragedies. We're not in this alone. It's people out there that will help us. They want to help. Just give Sarah a chance sweetie. Please. Do it for Mommy."

"Alright Mommy, I'll holla at Mrs. Berkowitz when I feel up to it.

I at least owe you that much. But the minute that she starts pulling out all kinds of different little instruments talking about '*Tell me what comes to your mind when you see this black sheet of paper*' or, '*Is this glass of water half empty or half full?*', I'm outta there," said Flower now laughing along with her mother.

"Okay sweetie. But promise me that you'll be nice and you'll give her a chance."

"I will. I promise," Flower smiled.

"That's my girl. Now give Mommy some sugar and I'll be on my way," said Mrs. Melinda leaning into her daughter.

Flower stopped her. "Maah. I'm fifteen, we don't call it sugar anymore."

"Girl please," said Mrs. Melinda as she leaned over and placed a comforting kiss on Flower's forehead.

As Mrs. Melinda got up to exit the bedroom, Flower called out to her mom. "Mommy."

"Yes dear," she said stopping at the bedroom door.

"I love you."

"I love you too," said her mom in a whisper as she shut the door behind herself.

Flower eased herself up underneath the covers as tears began rolling down her cheeks. She started thinking about the day that she came home from school and noticed her mother crying hysterically in the bathroom of their apartment. When her mom told her that Raymond had been killed, the tears began falling uncontrollably from Flower's eyes as well. But it wasn't because Raymond had been killed. Flower cried tears of happiness because she knew the molestation had finally come to an end. Her prayers had been answered at last.

After a thorough investigation, homicide detectives determined and explained what had happened to Mr. Raymond Abrams, Flower's father. On August 6, 1994, at approximately 1:30 p.m., Raymond apparently stopped off at a Spanish delicatessen to purchase his usual lunch, a turkey and provolone sandwich with mayonnaise on rye, and a Hawaiian Punch soft drink. Unbeknownst to him, an armed robbery was taking place, where two or three alleged gunmen barged into the bodega on the corner of 211th Street and White Plains Road. According to information gathered, one of the assailants shot the store's unarmed security guard off of a four-foot ladder that he used as his post near the entrance/exit door. The assailant then proceeded toward the counter where he gunned down two more employees near the store's cash register. While the assailants were cleaning out the register, Raymond entered the store and found himself in the worse predicament of his life. Raymond never had a chance to run. The lookout man who remained outside allowed Raymond to enter, preventing any chance of escape for the witness. The gunman then allegedly entered the store behind Raymond ambushing him, and putting six 40 caliber slugs into Raymond's head, neck and torso. He was pronounced dead at Montifore Medical Center about an hour after arrival. The information found in Raymond's wallet led the police to Mrs. Melinda Abrams. She was immediately notified and called in to identify the lifeless body of her husband. After almost losing her mind for a moment, she was escorted back home to wait for Flower and deliver her daughter the terrible news.

After Raymond's tragic death, Flower began having nightmares. She sometimes felt it was her fault that her father was dead because after their first sexual encounter, she prayed every night that God would stop him from abusing her. Deep down inside, Flower loved her father. She loved him to death apparently. Now her life has changed once again for the worse.

Flower's Bed

At 15 years old, Flower was now a beautiful young lady, very mature for her age and physically over-developed. She could pass for your average 21-year-old. At 5'5", 125 lbs., Flower's chocolate complexion and flawless skin gave off sort of a radiant type of vibe. It was like she was glowing without the shine. Her father had Indian in his blood which explained the long shiny hair that fell halfway down Flower's back. Her mother, on the other hand, was a natural beauty. She had soft skin, chinky eyes, and long eyelashes. Flower was her spitting image. Not only could Flower not keep her own father off of her, she had problems with almost all the boys in her neighborhood as well. She felt that if she shared herself with these guys, they would eventually fall in love with her. Her father once told her that and it stuck with her ever since.

CHAPTER TWO

7 a.m. the next morning …

The gentle tap at the door awakened Flower from her night's sleep. Tap! Tap! Tap! … Tap! Tap! Tap!

"Huh, who is it?" asked Flower, half asleep.

"It's me, Mommy," replied Mrs. Melinda, partially opening Flower's bedroom door. "I'm on my way to work now sweety. I just wanted to make sure that you were okay and whether or not you needed anything," she continued as she poked her head into Flower's room.

"No, I'm okay Mom. I'm fine. Thank you."

"Well alright then. And you should be getting up now and getting yourself ready for school. Come on now sweetheart. Up. Up."

"Okay Mom. I'm up." Flower ducked her head underneath her blanket.

"Flower. Come on. Now!"

"I'm up Mom. I'm up. … I'm up," she said, throwing the quilt to the floor.

"Alright now," said Mrs. Melinda as she closed the door.

Ring! Ring! Ring! Ring! The phone in Flower's room rang.

Flower's Bed

"Hello," said Flower.

"Yo, what's up?" said an unidentified voice.

"Who is this?" replied Flower, sitting up in her bed.

"Who does it sound like?"

"It sounds like I'm about to hang the fuck up on whoever the hell is playing on my damn phone this early in the morning. That's who it sounds like," said Flower with an attitude.

"Oh yeah, well check it. I'm going to hang up for a minute and when I call your ass back you better know who it is or this tennis bracelet I have in my hand is going to go on another bitch's wrist."

Click. The line went dead.

Ring! Ring! Ring! Ring! Ring!

"Hello," said Flower.

"Guess who?" said the now identified voice.

"Alize nigga," said Flower, confident of whom she was talking to now.

"I always knew diamonds were a girl's best friend. I just didn't think they could cure amnesia."

"Shut up nigga, I just woke up. My mind wasn't altogether at that moment. That's all. I knew who your ass was after I got my shit together," she said smiling.

"Yeah whatever."

"So what's up?" she asked.

"You. What are you doing?"

"I was asleep until your sexy ass woke me up."

Laughing, he thought to himself, "Now I'm sexy." Then he said, "So what do you have on?"

"My nightie, why?" she said bashfully.

"'Cause."

"Where are you?"

"I'm down the block."

"Down the block?" Flower seemed surprised.

"Yeah."

"With who, doing what?"

"I'm with my man. We're chilling." Alize tapped his friend and pointed at Mrs. Melinda as she drove by in her Maxima. "Yo, I'm trying to come through. What's up?"

Getting out of her bed, Flower said, "Why don't you give me a few minutes then."

"Just leave the door open and I'll let myself in. Alright?" said Alize.

"Ah-ight nigga."

Alize and his friend exited Alize's brand new customized black S500 Mercedes Benz. They walked halfway down the block and entered Flower's building. The two then got on the elevator and pressed seven.

"Yo, shorty better look good son," said J.R., Alize's friend. "And I hope that she's with it," he added.

"Be easy son. I got this. And have I ever fucked with anything less than a dime?" asked Alize, looking at his friend.

"Nah, and you have never shared any of your bitches either," said J.R. with a smirk.

"You're right, but shorty's a nympho. She told me that she fucked two dudes at the same time before so I guess today's your lucky day. Here we go," said Alize as they reached the seventh floor.

They exited the elevator to the right and entered Flower's apartment. "Son, sit right there," said Alize motioning his friend to have a seat in the living room. "I'll be right back," he added as he headed towards the bathroom where the shower was running. He walked into the bathroom and yanked the shower curtain open.

"Aaghh!" screamed Flower.

Laughing, Alize said, "You ain't been afraid of me."

Flower covered her chest and said, "Shut up nigga, you caught me off guard."

"Are you almost done?"

She smiled and said, "Yeah, give me a minute."

"I have a surprise for you," said Alize blushing.

"I know, my bracelet," said Flower blushing along with him.

"I have something else too."

"What?" asked Flower curious now.

"I'll show you when you come out. Just have your towel on, nothing else."

"Okay Boo." She finished up and dried herself off. As she walked out of the bathroom toward the living room, she noticed Alize and his friend watching television. She ducked back and called his name.

"Alize."

"Yo," he yelled.

"Come here."

Alize got up. "What's up?" he said, walking in her direction.

"Why didn't you tell me you had company with you?"

Alize shrugged his shoulders. "Because. He's the surprise."

"What?"

"Don't act like you're not with it. Like you're not fucking like that," said Alize looking her up and down.

"But I fucks who I want to fuck. Not who you want me to fuck," she said rolling her eyes.

He gazed at her with his bedroom eyes, then grabbed her and began French kissing her hard and deep. She eased herself into her bedroom with Alize attached to her and dropped her towel.

"Hold up," said Alize. "Let me put this on you." He pulled out a two-carat diamond tennis bracelet and placed it on her wrist. Flower smiled and dropped to her knees unzippering Alize's denim shorts like a child opening presents on Christmas day. She took his member into her warm mouth and pleasured him orally for the next few moments. He then removed his shirt and stepped out of his white on white Nikes along with his blue jean shorts. He sat at the edge of the bed, laid back and motioned Flower to straddle him reverse cowgirl style. She straddled him and began grinding like a dancer in a music video. As Flower's state of ecstacy hightened, Alize's friend, J.R., entered the room naked and approached the duo with his manhood pointing north. He began caressing Flower's breasts and French kissed her softly. After a few more moments, Alize repositioned Flower where she was now face to waist with him and her rear end was a target for J.R. The three of them explore one another's bodies for the next 90 minutes. When J.R.'s pager went off, he grabbed Flower's phone and exited the room.

"Alize," whispered Flower. She was lying beside him in her queen size bed.

"Huh."

"Did I make you feel good today Boo? Did I satisfy your sexy ass?" she said, pinching his butt softly.

He looked at her. "You always satisfy me Flow."

"I know, but I never did this with you before."

His gaze left her face. "I know, but you did your thing."

"You're not mad at me are you?"

Turning toward her and caressing her, he said, "Of course not Flow.

You made me feel really good today. Good looking out."

"Anything for you Boo," she smiled.

"Ayo Ze (pronounced Zay)," yelled J.R. standing at the door fully dressed.

"Who was that?" asked Alize.

"Peoples. Some people's need to be tooken care of, ya heard," said J.R. shouting from the living room.

"No doubt. Wait for me in the living room then," said Alize.

"Yeah, yeah. Yo Flower, you got it going on girl, ya heard. You need to stop playing and go and get that money though," said J.R. yelling from the front part of the apartment.

"Yeah ah-ight, I'll be out in a minute son," said Alize.

"Alright, bye Jay," said Flower.

"Listen cutie, I have to go and take care of some business. I'll holla at you later though. Ah-ight?" he said, kissing her on her forehead.

"Ah-ight."

"Was my man ah-ight Ma?" he asked.

"He was ah-ight. He didn't have to be poking me like he was crazy though," said Flower rubbing her stomach.

"Shiiit. Ya thang shouldn't be so good."

Flower smacked him gently on his shoulder. "Shut up. Go take care of your business and remember those shoes that I asked you about."

"I know, the sale will be over soon. I got you Ma."

Alize got dressed and headed for the living room.

"Come on son, we're out of here," said Alize as they both left with J.R. closing the door behind him. The duo took the stairs all the way to the lobby and left the building just as quietly as they came. As they approached the car, Alize told his friend, "Yo, just don't violate by trying to holla at shorty on some solo shit. She's a freak and all but she's still my people's. Shorty has been through crazy drama. So respect that. Ah-ight. I'm like her protector and shit, na mean?" said Alize.

"Yeah, yeah. I'm feeling you son," said J.R. He thought to himself, "I'm feeling shorty too," then he entered Alize's luxury sedan.

Alize stood 5'11" tall and his 215-pound frame looked thinner when he was fully clothed because he was very toned. His almond complexion was reminiscent of the sand at the beach and his curly hair complimented his pretty boy attitude. J.R. was also 5'11", but he was a deep brown like Flower was. He weighed 235 pounds and was much more huskier than Alize was. The two have been close since meeting up at the Bronx's House of Detention for Men, an adult temporary holding facility for inmates waiting to get transferred from the Bronx to Riker's Island, Queens. After their quick stints, the two hooked up, and though J.R. was from Fort Green, Brooklyn, and Alize was from the Bronx, business wise, these men were very compatible. Both were drug dealers and came from a similar background. However, one had aspirations of making money, getting out and going legit while the other said his life was the streets.

CHAPTER THREE

One week later …

169th Street & Washington Avenue, Claremont Projects …

Rosalyn walked over to Flower who was sitting on the hood of her mother's Nissan Maxima facing the oncoming traffic. As the late model cars raced west down 169th Street, passing Washington Avenue, Flower named every make and late model vehicle in her head. Each vehicle passed her by with a potential boyfriend behind the steering wheel.

"Excuse me hooker," said Rosalyn startling her best friend.

"Ros. What are you up to?" asked Flower turning around to acknowledge her friend.

"Nothing girl."

"Are those DKNY?" asked Flower pointing at Rosalyn's sneakers.

"Yeah," said Rosalyn looking at her brand new Donna Karan New York tennis shoes.

"Bitch, when did you get those?"

"Raheem bought them for me yesterday," said Rosalyn popping her bubble gum while she spoke.

"Are you going down on that boy Ros?" asked Flower.

"Girl, my middle name is Black & Decker, because I be sucking his trick ass dry." They both laughed.

"Not Mrs. Goodie Two Shoes who's always down my throat talking about 'fast ass Flower'."

"Flow, I only have one man. Unlike yourself who done been through everything in a Benz. Look at you. You're out here naming every car that drives by. That's a damn shame," said Rosalyn rolling her eyes.

"You're just jealous. You're mad because your butt is flatter than a one-month-old open soft drink. Nah, what's up girl?" said Flower as they continued laughing.

"You. So what's up with Alize? I hope you don't think he bought you that tennis bracelet for nothing. You know how niggaz are. They buy your ass something and the next thing you know, you're on a bus somewhere headed down south with the niggaz' drugs taped to your thighs. Either that or the nigga stashing his shit up in your apartment."

"Well you can count Alize out of that bunch. I told you Ros, he's more than just a fuck, the nigga cares about me," said Flower with a shimmy of her neck.

"Flow, you're 15. What the hell is a 21-year-old nigga that look as good as Alize and has as much money as Michael Jordan …"

"Donald Trump," said Flower interrupting her friend's lecture.

"Whatever," said Rosalyn. "But be for real. Listen Flow, you're my best friend and I will do anything for you. I will never hate on you. All I'm saying is that you really need to slow down. This dude probably has women crawling at his feet. I'm not saying that you're not good enough for him, I'm just saying be careful because guys be having other agendas. That's all."

"I feel you Ros, and I appreciate it. Hold up. Look Ros, you see that

Benz. That's a 1995 S400 right there. You could tell by the signal lights."

Rosalyn rolled her eyes. "You see what I mean!"

"Alright, alright, I hear you. I promise. I'll be careful."

"Flow, isn't that Alize's car right there?" said Rosalyn pointing to a black Mercedes Benz coming toward them.

Flower smacked her lips. "Yeah, that's my boo."

"Girl!"

"I know, I know, damn. I just get excited when I see his big dick ass."

The car rolled up and the tinted window on the driver's side rolled down.

"Hey cutie," said J.R.

"Oh hi, J.R. I thought you were Alize."

"He looks just as good," said Rosalyn mumbling next to Flower's ear.

"Nah, he's handling some business out of town right now. He'll be back in a couple of days. So who's your friend?" asked J.R.

"What? Who?"

"Me stupid," said Rosalyn smacking Flower on her shoulder.

"Oh, Ros. She's cool. Why?"

"Nothing, I'm just trying to be polite."

"Daamn! The nigga is cute and polite," said Rosalyn still whispering things into Flower's ear.

"Ayo Flower, let me holla at you for a minute. Get in," he said motioning with a jerk of his head.

"Ooohh," said Rosalyn, again being funny.

"Shut up girl. I'll be right back," said Flower making her way to the passenger side of the vehicle. She got in and J.R. pulled off and made the right onto Park Avenue. As the CD from the Rhythm and Blues group 'Total' played low in the background, J.R. began to speak.

"So what's up cutie?" he said keeping his eyes on the road.

"Nothing. I'm just chilling," said Flower.

He glanced at her. "You're looking good too," said J.R. with a devilish grin on his face.

"Thank you. And what made you decide to stop by?" said Flower, turning in her seat to face him.

"Well, I was in the neighborhood and I was thinking about you."

She licked her lips. "Oh really. Well what were you thinking about?"

"I was thinking, why would a beautiful girl like yourself not have a boyfriend." He looked over at her then placed his focus back on the road.

"Who said I don't have a boyfriend? And if I didn't, what makes you think I need one?"

He shrugged his shoulders. "Nobody said that you didn't have a boyfriend. I'm just assuming."

"You know what happens when people assume right?" said Flower with a sarcastic look on her face.

"Yeah, yeah, I know. You make an ass out of you and me," with the latter being said by both of them.

"Anyway, I wanted to ask you something if you don't mind."

"Before you say another word, let me clear something up first. The episode that happened between me, you and Alize is not something that I do everyday. Alize is my nigga and I was doing him a favor. So if that's what you had on your mind, forget about it." She rolled her eyes and turned back around in her seat.

"I apologize if I make it seem like I'm coming on to you, but that isn't what I'm here for."

"Oh." She sucked her teeth.

"I'm here to ask you have you ever thought about being in the entertainment industry?"

"What do you mean, like being a rapper or something?" she asked laughing.

He gave her a serious look. "No, I mean like dancing."

"In videos?"

"No, on stage."

"Stripping?" asked Flower with a puzzled look on her face.

"If that's the way you want to pronounce it. But people in the business choose to call it dancing. It's a little more classier in that sense I guess," said J.R. matter-of-factly.

"What sense? A stripper is a stripper, point blank."

Stuck at a red light, J.R. turned to Flower and said, "All I asked was have you ever thought about it. That's all. I mean you have a gorgeous body, a beautiful face, and those killer thighs may not be there in 15 years," he said looking down at her legs. "You might end up a single mom with a few children and on welfare. I just feel as a businessman, that you could make it in the entertainment field. I know plenty of women who have nice homes and are driving luxury cars just like this one, all from dancing. Now I'm not promising you anything, and I'm not forcing you to make a decision, all I'm saying is that you think about it. That's all."

"Well I don't know. I don't even know if I know how to dance."

"That won't be a problem. I know people who you can learn from. Well here we are," said J.R. as they pulled up in front of Flower's building where her friend Rosalyn was talking to her boyfriend Raheem.

"You just think about it gorgeous. As a matter of fact, here's my number," said J.R. handing Flower one of his cards. "I'm not going to be busy later on tonight. If you're free, give me a call. We'll talk some more. You know, over some food and champagne or something. Holla at me though. Ah-ight? Peace."

"Yeah ah-ight," said Flower as she exited the vehicle and slipped J.R.'s card into her pocket.

The car pulled off and Rosalyn never saw her friend pull up.

"Ros," yelled Flower.

"Hold up Flow. This nigga think he's slick," said Rosalyn referring to Raheem.

"Yeah ah-ight. Yo Flow, you better call your little comrade over here. Her ass is the one who thinks that she is slick. Always wanting money. Whenever you two get together, you guys are always up to something."

"Nigga stop fronting and give her some damn money. You're supposed to be a big baller anyway. So act like it nigga," said Flower.

"Yeah whatever," said Raheem passing Rosalyn some money.

"I'll holla at you two kitty cats later. And don't be jumping into any cars with out of town plates on them. You know what we do to those cats. Click, click! Let me hold that player. You won't be needing these keys for a while. And while you're at it, that watch, that bracelet, that chain, those rings and that bulge in your pocket, yeah, that too homie. Now walk your bitch ass to that corner and act like Jesse Owens because when I count to ten and your bama ass is still in my sight, you're going to say hello to my little friend. Yeah, that's how we do them," said Raheem who was all caught up in himself. He was illustrating with his hands how he robs people from out of town.

"Yeah right Raheem. Your ass won't even lick a stamp or peel a banana. That little 90 days that you did on Riker's Island shook your scared ass up. Get the fuck out of here," said Flower waving her hand.

Flower's Bed

"Whatever whore," said Raheem.

"Bitch," said Flower.

"Slut," continued Raheem as he walked away.

"Yo mama nigga! Fuck you!" she said raising her voice.

"Fuck you too! Broke bitch!"

"Ros, I hate his ass. Fat mothafucka!" said Flower who was being pushed away by her best friend.

"Just chill out Flow. Be easy. Now tell me about your little tour in the 500," said Rosalyn smiling.

"Girl, let me tell you, you're going to bug out. Let's walk to the store. I want a pickle. I'll tell you all about it as we walk."

The 5'6", 275 pound Raheem is Rosalyn's sugar daddy. He's a 26-year-old, light brown complexioned, easy going type of guy. He, Rosalyn and Flower have known one another for years. After returning home from a short prison stint and finding his girlfriend in a new relationship, Raheem decided that he'd had enough with older women. He accidentally got close with Rosalyn by having a long conversation with her outside their apartment building where he expressed the pain he was going through behind losing his girlfriend. The two then decided to go to the movies and afterwards had a bite to eat. They ended up in a motel room off of the Moshulu Parkway. And the two have been an item ever since. Raheem and Flower don't get along anymore because he feels Flower's promiscuity is going to rub off onto his little girlfriend and he'll eventually lose her too. Rosalyn and Flower have been best friends forever. No guy, as they promised one another, will ever come between them.

CHAPTER FOUR

Columbus, Ohio … The Eastside

Where Livingston and Champion Avenues meet, sets of row houses sit on either side of the street. Going further east, down Champion, lies a two-story, century old red, white and blue painted oakwood house. Inside, the atmosphere is gloomy. The half empty living room area was composed of one sofa, one matching Lazy Boy reclining chair and a 19" color television set that sat upon a small glass end table. The phone that lay in the center of the sofa began to ring.

Ring! Ring! Ring! Ring!

"Hello," said an unidentified voice.

"Yo, what's up?" asked Alize calling from his mobile phone.

"Shit. You. I'm hungry. I need a couple of pieces of chicken," said the man on the other end of the phone.

"Well check it, the food isn't ready yet. As soon as I fry up a little something, I'll holla back at you. Ah-ight?" said Alize.

"Ah-ight my dude, I'll be here kicking it."

Click. The line went dead.

Flower's Bed

"Aye homie, what's up with ol' boy from New York? Is he holding?" said another unidentified person in the living room of the house.

"Be cool fool. When I say I got it covered, then I got it covered, fool," said the guy who just got off the phone.

"Shit nigga, just let me shoot that New York nigga in his fucking head. I'm tired of them dudes coming out here charging us an arm and a leg for some drugs that have been cut a million times. Then they come down here and start fucking all of our ho's like we don't even exist or some shit. Ain't your boy Alize fucking with light skinned Monique from Sunbury Road?" asked the guy on the couch.

"Yeah fool."

"I've been trying to fuck Monique for years. Then this New York mothafucka pull up in his little Honda and his accent and he's fucking her in two days. Fuck him," said the guy on the sofa.

"Be cool Bear. Ol' boy said the car will be ready tomorrow. That way we can get his ass right. The cocaine and make a clean getaway."

Same night … New York City

As J.R. cruised up the West Side Highway in his own 1993 Mercedes Benz, his pager vibrated. He checked it and realized it's an unfamiliar number with the code 69. He called back and placed his car phone on speaker.

Ring! Ring! Ring!

"Hello," said Flower.

"Yo," said J.R. smiling.

"What's up? You probably don't even know who this is with all the women that you have."

"I know who this is, it's Flower. Your voice is too unique Boo. Where are you calling me from anyway?"

"I'm at home. I was just wondering when you were going to show me that club. By the way, what's the name of it and where is it located?"

"I see you've been doing a lot of thinking. Let me give you the rundown. The club is called The V.I.P. Club. It's located downtown Manhattan and it's very exclusive."

"What are you, one of their favorite loyal customers or something? How do you know so much about it?" asked Flower interrupting.

"Let's just say a favor for a favor was the deal and the favor owed to me wasn't worth my favor, so until I feel the scale is balanced, I have access to whomever and whatever I want on those premises. And knowing how exclusive this club is and how much money can be made, I thought about you and figured why let a beautiful girl like yourself get caught up in the streets. You know what I'm saying? Moving along, it's similar to other strip clubs, you can go topless or fully nude. Pole dance or lap dance, but the difference with this place is that everything is V.I.P. except the large stage. Anything goes. You keep your tips, but you pay a weekly fee to the owner. But in your case, you don't pay anything to anyone so you reap all of your benefits. The customers are of all races and cultures. Trust me girl, you'll make a whole lot of money."

"So where are you at now?" asked Flower.

"I'm about ten minutes from your crib. Do you want to go and see the spot right now?"

"Hell yeah," she said excitedly.

"Ah-ight, meet me downstairs in like ten minutes."

"Okay."

Click. The line went dead.

As J.R. arrived and pulled up in front of the deserted building, Flower came walking out in an all black cat suit and got into the car.

"Damn shorty. Okay, okay, trying to make a very good impression I see." He was thinking about the episode they shared the week before.

"Well you're looking good yourself J.R."

They pulled off and headed for the highway.

"Listen Flow, I have to make one quick stop first, then we can go and look at your future," said J.R. with a smile.

The couple pulled up to the Tracy Towers apartment complex on Jerome Avenue in the Bronx.

"Is this where you live at J.R.?" asked Flower, looking out the window of the car up toward the roof of the building.

"This is one of my places, why? You know someone who lives in the Towers too?"

"No, just asking."

"Well come on, I'm trying to hurry up. I'm just as anxious as you are."

The duo exited the vehicle and walked inside one of the towers. They reached J.R.'s 27th floor apartment and Flower was amazed at how beautiful and exquisite his place was. Chandeliers, wall to wall carpeting. Paintings hanging everywhere.

"This place is really nice J.R. Do you live here alone?" she asked examining his living quarters.

J.R. stood rocking back and forth with his hands clasped behind his back. He replied, "Yup! You like it?"

"Hell yeah."

"You'll be able to afford something like this if you play your cards right. So just give me like twenty minutes to freshen up. Make yourself at home."

J.R. walked to the rear of his apartment and disappeared.

Flower carefully toured the apartment, going from the living room, to the dining room and then into the kitchen area, picking up and pocketing a Gucci keychain pouch. Thinking to herself, "This keychain is nice. I could use this for myself." She made her way to the rear of the apartment and peered through an ajar bedroom door where she saw J.R. lotioning his naked body.

"Damn. I didn't realize he was that fine when he was fucking me," she thought to herself.

J.R. turned around giving Flower a better view of his half stiff member. She opened the door to his surprise, walked over to him, pushed him on the bed and sucked him to full erectness. After a few minutes of looking like she was bobbing for apples, Flower stood up and said, "Ever see a cat suit do this?" She revealed a slit in her crotch area secured by Velcro. She positioned herself on top of him and rode him like the Lone Ranger. The two of them reached their orgasms simultaneously and just as smoothly as Flower straddled him, she climbed up off of him and walked into his master bathroom and cleaned herself up. J.R. continued to lay there enjoying the after shocks of his own orgasm. After getting his thoughts together, he cleaned himself up and the two of them headed for the V.I.P. Club.

The phone rang … Columbus, Ohio

Ring! Ring!

"Hello," said an unidentified voice.

"Yo, is Bear there?" asked Alize.

"Aye, hold on … Aye, Bee Shizzle! … Yo Bee Shizzle!" shouted the unidentified male.

"Yo," replied Bear. He was busy rolling marijuana.

"Your dude is on the phone," said the guy, holding the telephone out to Bear.

"What dude?"

"Ya boy from up top." He nodded and gave Bear a facial expression that said, "This is our vic."

"Ah-ight. Tell him I said hold on." Bear dropped the reefer and picked up his cellular phone.

"Aye, Ze, he said hold on."

"I heard him."

New York City …

Ring! Ring! Ring!

Over the loud music that blared from the club's speakers, J.R. felt his cellular phone vibrating.

"Flow, give me a minute. Matter of fact, meet me at the bar in a minute," said J.R.

"Okay," replied Flower. She found her way to the bar.

"Yo," said J.R. answering his phone.

"Aye, this fool just called back. He might want to do something now. The car ain't even ready yet," said the unidentified voice.

"What do you want us to do if he wants to meet now?" he added.

"Damn. Damn, damn, damn," said J.R. "Fuck it, do what you're getting paid to do. But be careful because son keeps that thing on him at all times," said J.R. referring to a firearm.

"Aye man, can't we just kill that fool over here?"

"Shut the fuck up. Why the fuck are you talking like that over the phone? I'll call your ass back," shouted J.R.

Click. J.R.'s line went dead.

"Did you get that chief?" said DEA agent Jack Samuels.

"Sure did," said Chief John Ross of the New York Drug Enforcement Agency. "Trace that call. It's a 614 area code again. That's his crew in Ohio. Get somebody on them immediately before Alize turns up a dead man."

Ring! Ring!

"Hello," said Bear.

"You fucking idiot. I was on my cell phone. I told you we never talk like that unless we're on a land line or face to face," said J.R.

"So what's up?" asked Bear.

"Call that shit off now." J.R. was fuming.

"Shit, my boys done went to meet him. They found out that the car was ready so they went to pick up the car first, then they're going to meet your boy at the Food Market on Livingston Avenue and James Road, out east."

"Damn. I'll holla back. I have to think," said J.R.

Click. J.R.'s line went dead.

Click. Bear's line went dead.

Click. The DEA's line went dead.

"Samuels, get your people in Ohio set up at that location. As soon as they spot those kids, bring 'em down," said Ross.

"10-4 Chief."

The V.I.P. Club … New York City …

"Boo what's up. You look stressed," said Flower.

"Nah, I'm ah-ight. I'm just a little tired you know. You did drain me before we came here. Remember?" said J.R. with a smile.

"No you drained me," said Flower with her sexy smile. "Here, have some Amaretto. It's a sour. The lemon/lime mix always puts me in the mood," she added.

J.R. gulped down the drink and proceeded to show Flower around introducing her to the club owner, Mr. Tony Ciocca, floor manager Bill Whitney, bartenders Joey Garcia and Joey Padeo. And the club's sexy dancers.

Columbus, Ohio …

Livingston Avenue and James Road …

"Aye fool, here he comes right now," said Ness to BG who was in the trunk of their four-door Bonneville with a loaded 30-30 Winchester. A hole was drilled into the rear of the trunk leaving room for the rifle's nose to be fired from. "Ayo, you ready fool?"

"Yeah nigga, just go and handle your business. And stay out of my way," said BG tucked uncomfortably in the trunk.

One mile down Livingston Avenue, Columbus, Ohio police raced toward the intersection of Livingston and James.

"Aye Ze, what's up?" said Ness, giving Alize a handshake.

"Shit. What's up with you? Y'all niggaz doing it big asking for fifteen of them things. The last time I saw y'all, y'all only bought two of 'em," said Alize sitting on the hood of his 1993 four-door Honda Accord.

"I know, but we copping for somebody else too."

"Oh yeah? Well put your fucking hands up above your head then," said Alize pointing a 9mm semi-automatic Ruger at Ness' face.

"Damn Homie. What's up?" asked Ness, expecting Alize to do that.

"Just checking. Y'all bama ass niggas ain't as dumb as people think," said Alize searching Ness.

As the local police turned south onto James Road, one of the patrol car's tire screeched startling Alize. As soon as Alize turned to find out what car was screeching, a shot rang out from the trunk of the Bonneville ripping through Alize's forehead killing him instantly. He dropped to the floor and Ness began to run toward the Bonneville with the Columbus police right behind him. The Bonneville was cornered off. With all the blinding lights in his face, all Ness heard was "Don't fucking move."

The V.I.P. Club …

New York City …

"Excuse me," said J.R. bumping into a patron in the crowded club.

"No, excuse me," said Chief DEA Agent Ross, smiling at J.R. "Would you come with me sir," he said with the assistance of Agent Samuels and Agent Johnson.

As they exited the club, another agent passed Chief Ross the phone. After a short pause, Chief Ross looked over at J.R. and said, "Javon Richardson, you're under arrest for murder, conspiracy to commit murder, drug trafficking, money laundering and a whole list of other shit that I'm going to put together on you. You're friend Alize is dead, and we got the clowns you had pull the trigger. You have the right to remain silent. Anything you say or do can and will definitely be used against you in a Federal Court of Law. Yeah it's Federal. We've been watching you for fourteen months. You have the right to an attorney. You won't be able to afford one once we confiscate all of your shit so one will be appointed to you. Now get this piece of shit out of here," said Ross to his fellow officers. The arresting officers handcuffed J.R. and brought him outside. As they put him into the squad car, Agent Samuels said to Agent Ross, "What about the girl?"

"She's harmless, leave her be. I'm quite sure pretty boy here hooked her up with someone already anyway."

Flower's Bed

CHAPTER FIVE

The yellow taxicab pulled up in front of 450 East 169th Street. Flower handed the Nigerian cab driver a crisp $20 bill and told him to keep the change. She reached her apartment and quietly entered without waking up her mother. Flower walked into her room, turned on her night light and began getting undressed. She picked up her phone and listened to the two messages that Rosalyn left her. One of the messages was, "Flow, this is Ros, call me when you get in." Beep! And the second message said, "Flower, you done blossomed once again. You go girl! Work the middle! Tell me all the details mama. Bye." Beep!

Flower clicked the receiver and dialed Rosalyn's number.

Ring. Ri...

"Hello," said Rosalyn in a half asleep whisper.

"Chickenhead," said Flower, calling her best friend a hoochie mama in another term.

"What's up girl? You finally brought your ass home. I guess the dick was all that," said Rosalyn smiling.

"Bingo," said Flower laughing. "Hey, are you going to school tomorrow?"

"Hell yeah girl. I need all of my credits to graduate."

"Well I'll see you on our way to school tomorrow. I'll tell you all about it then okay?"

"What did you do, find some dirt on ol' boy?"

"Nope. I think I found a new hustle."

"Flower!"

"What?"

"Bitch, you better not …" Flower cut her off.

"I'll holla at your tomorrow. I'll be out front at 7:30 a.m."

Click. The line went dead.

Rosalyn rolled back over, placed her hand on her forehead and said very softly to herself, "I hope my girl is not doing anything stupid."

Since entering high school a little over one year ago, Flower and Rosalyn had begun utilizing the Bx 41 bus as their main source of travel to and from school. Every morning, the girls get on the bus at 169th Street and Webster Avenue and ride north on Webster Avenue for about four miles until they reach Gunhill Road. The bus then makes a right and heads east on Gunhill Road for about one half mile until it reaches White Plains Road. At White Plains Road, the two young ladies exit the bus and continue walking east on Gunhill Road until they reach Evander Childs High School on the corner of Barnes and Bronxwood Avenues. Outside of the school, teenagers from all over the neighborhood engage in personal activities. Flower and Rosalyn stand at the bottom of the school steps engaged in their own conversation.

The next morning …

"So he just left you in the club like that?" asked Rosalyn.

"Yup. It's all good though. I understand that him and Alize are always busy. He probably had to take care of some business or something," said Flower.

"Some business, Bitch, he slid off with another bitch! Don't no nigga just leave a potential piece of ass unless they're tending to another piece of potential ass. And to top it off, you had to ask the manager for carfare to get home. His fake ass is probably broke," said Rosalyn rolling her eyes and sucking her teeth.

"Well his car and his crib tell me otherwise. He's just another piece of dick anyway. But like I said, I peeped out that whole club scene. Them bitches that were dancing in there were beautiful, but they couldn't shake it like I could. I'm telling you Ros, as soon as J.R. gives me the okay and I straighten it out with Alize, I'm going to have that club on lock down. I'll show some rich ass nigga the true meaning of V.I.P."

Bliiing! Bliiing! Bliiing! The school bell rang.

"Oh shit, Flow, I left my calculator on my dresser. We got a math test first period, remember?"

"Damn Ros. I forgot about that damn test. I have my calculator with me so we should be okay."

"Let's go. Come on," said Rosalyn as the girls rushed to their first period class.

Third period, Study Hall ...

"Ros, don't worry about it. We did good. I triple checked all of our answers," said Flower.

"How?" asked Rosalyn.

"The nerd bitch next to me."

Confused, Rosalyn asked, "What?"

"Jenny Jones. The Jenny Jones look alike from Weschester County. That bitch be acing all of her tests. I had my circles darkened before she had her own darkened," said Flower as both girls began laughing.

"Excuse me," said a female student hall monitor. "Is there a Flower

Abrams in here?" The school monitor was looking at everyone in the room.

Flower and Rosalyn looked at each other. "Right here, why?" asked Flower firmly.

"You're requested at the Guidance Counselor's Office," said the young lady before walking off.

"Flow, what's that all about?" asked Rosalyn, being nosy.

"I don't know. My ass been with you all morning."

"Let's go then."

"Come on," said Flower.

The girls got to the guidance office and Flower immediately noticed Mrs. Sarah Berkowitz, her family counselor. Through gritted teeth, Flower asked herself, "What is she doing here?"

"Who's that, your P.O.?" asked Rosalyn with a smirk on her face.

"No stupid, that's my family counselor, Mrs. Berkowitz. My mom has been stressing me lately about having an interview with this lady. She thinks that I may need someone to talk to about my father's death."

"Do you?"

"Hell no."

"Did you tell your mother that?" said Rosalyn opening a piece of bubble gum.

"Yeah, but she insisted and I agreed, so I guess I'll be 'The Silence of the Lamb' for the next half hour."

"Knock yourself out Flow. But don't fuck with her because if she diagnoses your ass with something, (demonstrating an up and down zippering motion), it's the Straight Jacket for you."

"Fuck it, if Ol' Dirty Bastard of the Wu Tang Clan can survive, so can I," said Flower walking into the office, greeting Mrs. Berkowitz with a hand shake.

Flower's Bed

"Good morning Flower. How are you doing today?" said Mrs. Berkowitz.

"I'm fine, and yourself?" asked Flower responding nicely.

"Have a seat darling."

"Thank you." Flower took a seat across from Mrs. Berkowitz.

"Flower, I hope I didn't interrupt anything important and I apologize for barging in on you at your school, but I use to work here and I figured it would be a great opportunity to get up with you as well as visit some of my old friends and coworkers."

"You didn't interrupt anything, and it was no problem stopping by."

"Well since that's settled, why don't we begin," said Mrs. Berkowitz rustling with some papers.

"Begin what?" Flower looked surprised.

"Oh, I'm sorry. I sound like a psyche, don't I?" said Sarah tapping Flower lightly on her hand. "You know what, why don't I begin by letting you know a little bit about myself and how your mom and I met and so on and so forth. Is that alright with you?" asked Sarah smiling.

"Sure Mrs. Berkowitz. Be my guest."

For the next thirty minutes or so, Mrs. Berkowitz summarized her childhood, her teenage years, and her young adulthood to Flower. Before she could get into the deep relationship that she has with Melinda, Flower's mom, the bell rang, ending the period and their session.

"Aaww! I hope I didn't bore you with my life. I would really like to get to know you a little bit better Flower, so if we can arrange something for the future, I'll be more than happy to lend you my ear," said Mrs. Berkowitz.

"You didn't bore me Mrs. Berkowitz, I enjoyed hearing about your life. Anytime. In fact, when I get home today, I'll let my mom know that I had an interesting time with you and I'll also let her know that I look forward to seeing you again."

With a smile on her face, Mrs. Berkowitz looked at Flower and said, "Good. Very good. Thank God."

Flower got up and offered Mrs. Berkowitz her hand and told her goodbye.

Flower eventually met back up with Rosalyn and shared with her the encounter she had with Mrs. Berkowitz. Rosalyn made all kinds of jokes with Flower about how she's 'The One Who Flew Over the Cookoo's Nest,' and how she's one of 'The Twelve Monkeys,' referring to two movies involving people who seemed crazy. The pair rode home together as usual and before parting from one another, they let each other know that they'll be on the phone talking again before the night was over.

In front of Flower's apartment …

"Alright, bye hoochie," said Rosalyn.

"Where are you going? To Raheem's house?" asked Flower.

"Yeah, I should be over there for a few hours. Flow, ain't that your phone ringing?" asked Rosalyn, leaning close to Flower's door.

Realizing herself, Flower began unlocking her door.

"Ros, I'll holla at you later."

"Ah-ight."

Flower entered her apartment and answered the phone. "Hello," she said.

"This is a V.A.C. prepaid call. You will not be charged for this call. This call is from 'J.R.' If you would like to accept this call, press '5' now. If you would like to decline the call, hang up now. If you …"

Beeep! Flower pressed '5'. "Hello," she said.

"Hello," said J.R.

Flower's Bed

"J.R. Where are you? Are you in jail?"

"Yeah."

"Well where's Alize, does he know?" Flower sounded concerned.

"You know what, I have no idea where Ze is at. I've been trying to call him all day. Anyway, how are you doing? What's up with you?"

"I'm okay. How are you doing?"

"Aye, I'm straight."

"Are you going to get bailed out?"

"These people got me on some trumped up bullshit ass charges. So I don't have a bail just yet. I plan on getting out soon though. As soon as I get with my lawyer, I should be ah-ight."

"Well if you need me to do anything for you, just let me know."

"I appreciate that Flow. Listen, just go back to the club and make that money girl. Okay?"

"Okay."

"I'll call you back when I can."

"Alright."

"Ah-ight, bye."

"Bye."

Click.

Over at Raheems' house …

"Mmtwa! Mmtwa! Mmtwa!"

"Damn Rah, that shit feels so good," said Rosalyn.

"I know Boo. Just let me do me," said Raheem sucking on Rosalyn's feet.

"Boo."

"Huh Rah," said Rosalyn gripping her sheets.

"You heard about Alize right?"

She was panting. "No, what happened? Did he get locked up or something?"

"Nah, homie is dead."

"Dead! What?" said Rosalyn sitting up on Raheem's bed naked, nipples looking like two 45 caliber bullets.

"Yeah, dude got killed out of town. Somewhere in Ohio, niggas smoked him."

"What? When?"

"I think like a few days ago."

"How Rah? Who? Why?" She placed her hand over her mouth.

"I don't know. But word on the streets is that his man J.R. had him set up for the kill. Probably trying to rob him or something. When you're dealing with long paper like they were, envy and jealousy can come between a relationship."

"So where's J.R. now? Are the cops looking for him?"

"J.R. is downtown at the Federal county jail in Manhattan. I guess since it happened out of town, crossing state lines made it Federal. I really don't have all the facts yet. Like I said, that's just word on the streets. Now lay back and let me lick my way north until I come to the fork in the road. Know what I mean?" said Raheem with a smile.

Rosalyn thought for a second, then laid back down and floated back into a state of ecstasy.

One hour later …

The phone rings …

Ring! Ring! Ring!

"Hello," said Flower.

Flower's Bed

"Flow, did you hear what happened with J.R. and them?" asked Rosalyn, eager to spread the news.

"Yeah, he called me earlier. How did you find out?"

"Raheem told me."

"That fat mother fucker is always in someone else's business."

"Aaannd! He's still my man," said Rosalyn sucking her teeth.

Flower rolled her eyes as she twirled her hair. "Yeah whatever. What's up though?"

"Girl, you act like shit don't stink."

"What are you talking about Ros?"

"Alize. I'm talking about your so-called love."

"I told you, he's my Boo. He loves me for real. He just need to slow it down or I might end up with his friend," said Flower examining her freshly painted fingernails.

"You really don't know, do you?" said Rosalyn.

"What, that he's fucking other bitches? What Ros? What is it? He tried to get with you too or something? What? I hate it when you get quiet on me like that. Is everything okay?"

"I'm okay … Flower?"

"What Ros? Just tell me what's going on."

"Flow, Alize is dead!" said Rosalyn firmly.

"What?" said Flower, the news not sinking in yet.

"And J.R. is in jail because of it!"

"Nooooo!" screamed Flower as she dropped the phone.

CHAPTER SIX

That night, Flower mourned the loss of the only guy she felt truly loved her. In her eyes, Alize was her knight in shining armor. From the time that they met, it seemed like true love. Flower had just turned fourteen and by then had grown out of having birthday parties. On this one particular day, her father had been trying to lure her somewhere secluded so the two could engage in sexual intercourse. Flower gave her mom an excuse, saying it loud enough so that her father could hear, hoping that it could buy her some time to avoid the encounter altogether. She told her mom that she was going to the store and would be right back. She made it only a few yards from the entrance of her building before the tears began rolling down her soft precious cheeks. She stopped at the corner of 169th Street and Park Avenue and decided to sit on a parked car when she noticed the car she was sitting on was occupied.

"I'm sorry sir," said Flower, with tears still flowing down her cute face.

Opening the door, Alize stepped out of the car and asked if she was okay. "Ayo shorty, you ah-ight?"

"Yeah, I'm okay," said Flower holding herself like if it were cold outside.

Stepping closer, he noticed that she was a resident in his neighborhood. "Who dat, Flower?"

"Yes," she said, wiping the tears from her eyes.

"Nah, you ain't ah-ight. What happened to you? Where your people's at?" said Alize referring to her family members.

Alize always thought that being ghetto would make him seem more aggressive than he really was. Speaking it was second nature for him.

"My family is upstairs. I'm okay, really."

"Oh, you don't want to talk about it. It's cool. Do you need anything while you're out here crying your heart out?"

"I want a drink," said Flower, not sounding too sure.

"A drink? What do you want to drink other than alcohol?"

"I want a 40 oz.," said Flower referring to a bottle of beer.

"I just said, except alcohol. You must think you're grown and every time you have a problem, you're going to drink your misery away. Well it don't work that way."

She shrugged her shoulders. "I know, I'm just thirsty."

"Thirsty, okay, drink some of this," said Alize passing Flower a bottle of Evian water.

"Thank you." She took a sip. "What were you doing sitting here in the dark?"

"I was waiting for someone."

A tiny smile crept on her face as she moved the hair that covered her left eye. "Who, your girlfriend?"

"Nah, I ain't got no girl. Ho's ain't nothing but trouble."

"What kind of trouble?" Flower was very inquisitive. She wanted to know.

Leaning on the hood of his car, Alize began to speak. "I'm saying, you know, always sweating a nigga. A nigga don't need that shit when he out here hustling. Risking his life ayeday to feed the homefront. I mean, fuck, so what! What if I did want a different piece of pussy every now and then that didn't mean anything to me except a little one hundred dollars and a pack of condoms? But you're home, you mean the world to me and I'm buying you diamonds and furs. I got you sitting up in a plushed out crib, pushing luxury cars, hair done every week. Nails done every week and access to cash whenever you need it. But then you want to ask me, 'Where you been at nigga?' Fuck up outta here," said Alize demonstrating with a wave of his hand. "Niggas don't be trying to hear that shit. It's bad enough, we're out here worrying about whether or not niggas is the police or if we're flooding the streets with good shit. So that's why I don't need no bitch under me. Face down, ass up, that's my motto." He crossed his arms.

"Okay," said Flower.

"Okay?"

"Mm hmm. You made your point. I respect that. I may not necessarily agree with your motto, but it's real so I respect it."

"Oh."

"What's your name anyway, Mr. Face-Down-Ass Up?"

"Alize. But my mans and them call me Ze. You know, short for Alize."

"Duh."

"So since I basically ran down to you my problems or at least my outlook on things, maybe you'd like to share with me why you were crying a little while ago."

"Did you eat yet?" she asked.

"Why, are you hungry?"

"Mm hmm." Flower nodded her head.

"What do you want to eat?" said Alize walking back over to the driver's side of the vehicle.

Getting into the passenger seat, Flower responded, "I don't know, anything."

"Well what is it that you like to eat?"

"I eat everything I guess. Chicken, French fries, cheeseburgers." She shrugged her shoulders.

"Ah-ight, ah-ight, I got you. We're going to shoot down to Willies."

"What's Willies?"

"You don't know about Willie Burger's? Shiiit! That's that famous hamburger stand on 145th Street and 8th Avenue in Harlem. Dude owns a spot called Willie's Lounge that's right next to it too. That spot is for all of the ol' heads. His burger stand got the bomb turkey burgers. I don't eat that beef shit. Never did. My pops ain't play that. He told me that black people have the highest death rate with heart disease. You know, high cholesterol, high blood pressure, strokes, heart attacks. Shit like that. And all that greasy red meat shit will make us get all of that shit so I've stayed away from it all of my life. I don't smoke either. I do drink though," he said smiling.

Flower touched Alize's hand. "Wait, before we pull off, do you have Mary J. Blige's tape?"

"Hell yeah. Shorty is from Yonkers. I have to represent for shorty. Yonkers to us is just like Harlem is to us, it's basically all one borough. It's past 110th Street going downtown or past Yonkers going Upstate that separates us."

Fifteen minutes later ...

They reached Willie Burger's and after ordering, decided to go ten blocks up to 155th Street, The Pologrounds basketball court, also known as

Rucker Park. It's Harlem's most famous basketball court. They sat and chatted about all kinds of things for hours. The time flew by. When they ran out of things to say, Alize got out of the car and said, "Hold on."

"What are you doing?" asked Flow.

"I'm about to take a piss, hold up." Alize walked to the rear of his car and unzippered his pants.

As he urinated, Flower sat there amazed at how daring he was. In fact, it turned her on. Alize got back into the car and caught eye contact with Flower.

"What?" said Flower trying not to look Alize directly in his eyes.

"Damn yo, you're mad cute. I didn't even realize you were so pretty."

"You really think I'm pretty?" She was blushing from ear to ear.

"Hell yeah," said Alize keeping his eyes drawn to hers.

Alize leaned over and began kissing Flower. Kissing him back, Flower started fiddling with Alize's belt managing to get his pants loose and her hands on his penis. Enjoying it, Alize immediately became erect and repositioned himself so that his member looked as though it was trying to touch the sunroof of his 1990 Acura Legend. Looking into Alize's eyes, Flower began stroking his rod up and down gently.

"Hold up," said Alize. "Take one leg out of your joints," he continued, referring to Flower's pants.

After removing one leg from out of her sweat pants and panties, Alize adjusted the seats back and positioned Flower so that they could perform in the missionary position. Alize got on top of Flower and entered her slowly.

"Damn. What the!" said Alize, gasping over how good it felt inside of her.

"What. What's up?"

"Nothing, this shit is mad good. Mmmph! Mmmph! Mmmph! Mmmph! Mmmph!" moaned Alize as he picked up his pace stroking her.

"Ooooh! Ooooh! Ooooh! Ooooh! Ooooh! Ooooh!" responded Flower, meeting Alize's every thrust with her own.

"Oooh yeah! Damn! This feels so good yo!" said Alize stroking away.

"Ooooh yeah! Don't stop! Mmmmph! It feels good inside of me too. Don't cum yet Ze. Don't cum! Keep going. Keep going Ze," continued Flower.

"Ooooh! Ooooh! Ooooh! Said Alize speeding up.

After about ten minutes of intense stroking, Alize felt himself beginning to ejaculate. Grabbing Flower by her waist, he dug himself deep into her for his final few strokes and held her tightly against himself on his last stroke for about ten seconds, releasing everything he had inside of her. He pulled out and collapsed back into the driver's seat of the fogged up sedan.

"Whoa! Damn! Word up! What the!" said Alize enjoying the after effects of their intense sexual encounter.

After pulling up her clothing, Flower began talking. "So?"

"So what?" asked Alize.

"We're still cool right?" she asked bashfully.

"Yeah, hell yeah. Why?"

"You know, face down, ass up," said Flower smiling.

"Listen, I know I said all of that."

Cutting him off, Flower said, "It's okay, I knew what I was getting myself into."

"Nah, listen. Getting to know you, talking to you and all, that was fun. I haven't done anything like that in a long time. I enjoyed myself tonight. Really."

"I bet you did," said Flower smiling.

"I did, really. I mean the entire time we spent together, I was comfortable. I felt at ease. You never know, in another year or so, you could be wifey material, getting diamonds and all that from the kid."

"Why in another year, why not now?" She crossed her arms and rolled her eyes.

"Because, you should be around eighteen by then right? You're at least seventeen now, or I don't know, maybe you're eighteen, or will be eighteen sooner than one year. Right?"

Flower just looked at him.

"Right Flower?" he added with a firmer tone. "Talk to me."

"I'm fourteen Alize." She shimmied her neck.

"What! Get the fuck outta here. You ain't no fourteen. You can't be. Look at how big your ass is. Look at your face, and your hair. Look at how you talk."

"I'm fourteen. I am."

"How could you do this to me? I'm not no child molester." Alize slapped himself lightly and rubbed his face from his forehead down to his lips.

"I know you're not."

"So why didn't you say anything or at least try and stop me?"

"Because, it doesn't matter to me. Age isn't an issue with me. It never has been." She looked away from him.

"What! What are you talking about age ain't an issue with you? You be fucking like that? With older guys?"

She looked at him then looked away again. "No, older guys do it with me."

"What, you selling pussy to older men?"

"No. I don't sell my coochie. And you're saying men, like it's a whole lot." Again, she looked at Alize and rolled her eyes.

"Hold up. Hold up. Let's back this thing up for a second. Correct me if I'm wrong. You're fourteen years old, correct?"

"Yup."

"And you weren't a virgin before tonight, correct?"

"Correct."

"You've had plenty of sex before, right?"

"Yup," said Flower still looking Alize directly in his eyes.

"You've had sex with older men?"

"Older man."

"Oh, only one?"

"Yup."

"But you said older guys did it to you?"

"Nope. I said one older guy do it to me."

"Okay, one older guy does it to you."

"Yup."

"Is he your boyfriend?"

"Nope."

"Is he your friend at all?"

"Sort of, but he doesn't act like it."

"Does he pay you to have sex with him?"

"No, I told you, I don't sell my coochie."

"What, you just give it to him?"

"No."

"Does he take it from you?"

"Yup."

"He takes it from you!?" Alize was getting upset.

"Yeah."

"I'm not with that telling on a nigga shit, but you're different. You're a girl and you're not in the street life so you can do shit like tell on niggas and get away with it."

"So?"

"So why isn't this guy in jail?"

"I don't think he deserves to go to prison."

"Why not? He's taking your pussy against your will isn't he?"

"Yeah."

"So the nigga should be in jail or shot the fuck up or something."

"It's my fault though."

"What! How the hell is it your fault?"

"Because."

"Because what?"

"Because I allowed it to happen over and over again without saying anything. People are going to think that I wanted it to happen." Flowers eyes began to water.

"No they wouldn't. And what the fuck do allowing it to continue going on for a particular length of time have to do with whether it's wrong or not. If you didn't consent to it, it's wrong and it's a crime. Did you consent to it?"

"No."

"Then it's a crime."

"I just can't." Her lips were trembling.

"Don't ever say that you can't, Flower. You know why?"

"Why?" she bellowed.

"Because that word doesn't exist. But you can stop this man from sexually abusing you."

"No I can't!"

"Why not?"

"Because he won't stop!" said Flower beginning to cry.

"Why won't he stop Flower? Why can't you stop this man from sexually abusing you?"

"Because he's my father!" said Flower, the tears flowing heavily down her face.

Leaning his head back on his headrest, Alize's thoughts went one direction. "If I ever get the chance, I'm going to kill that mothafucka!"

Ever since then, Alize became Flower's significant other in a sense. They weren't officially titled boyfriend and girlfriend and were both allowed to see other parties, but in Flower's mind, Alize was her man. In his mind, however, Flower was like his little sister and he vowed to protect her by any means. He promised himself that one day he'd get enough courage to free Flower from her notorious father.

CHAPTER SEVEN

Midnight at The V.I.P Club …

It's Friday, the atmosphere is party, party, party! Women of all colors, shapes, sizes, races and ages entertained men and women alike of all different kinds. Dance music played loud throughout the club's 20 some odd speakers equipped with a surround sound. Before Flower made her move for the dressing room, she checked out the scenery. A few feet from the entrance a busty white woman dressed in a denim bikini stood in a designated smoking area occupied by two small round tables with four seats pulled up to each table. Smoking on a Virginia Slim cigarette, she gave a heavyset black guy a lap dance and blew smoke in his face apparently for his pleasure. Walking ahead another ten feet, V.I.P. booths that resembled dressing rooms were lined side by side one another with all of their curtains drawn indicating their usage. To the right, Flower saw the bar area. It's the weekend so she knew that every girl in the club was doing her best to shake what their mothers gave them. Flower saw some of the girls that she met the one night she came to the club with J.R. The girls all walked around giving one another fake smiles and fake hand waves. A few of the featured girls raced back and forth like they're in a rush to go somewhere. Every so often, one of the featured girls was a no-show leaving a slot available for any locals willing to showcase their talent. Flower headed for the bar and ordered a drink.

"May I have a Sex on the Beach, Joey?" she asked keeping her eyes focused on the customers that roamed the club and occasionally disappeared inside the small booths.

"Sure," said the bartender.

Over the noise, the bartender lets Flower know that all of her drinks are on the house. She drank half of what she ordered and left the rest on the counter. Flower made her way to the dressing room where several dancers were freshening up. All the ladies were in thongs, topless or nude.

"Girl, it is rocking out there tonight," said Cinnamon, a tall caramel complexioned dancer with a large butt wearing a blond wig.

"Who you telling? I made $75 in forty minutes," said Cherry, a short redbone with short curly black hair, a petite build and a wide gap between her legs.

"Any of your regulars here tonight?" asked Cinnamon.

"Smokey. His ass must've gotten paid today because those dollars seem to be coming out of everywhere," replied Cherry.

"Girl, you give him some yet?" asked Mt. Everchest, a six foot white amazon hillbilly with huge breasts and large legs.

"Eve, I don't have to give him any. By the time we get into the second song of my super grinding, he's already shooting in his pants. So I imagine how quick he'd cum if I gave him some."

"Shit, I wish I could find me a guy who would fuck me for ninety seconds and give me $100 for it. I'd be the richest bitch in the east," said Everchest.

"Girl, you have to find somebody to climb your big ass first," said Cinnamon, causing laughter amongst all of the girls, including Flower.

"Aye, did I tell you all about the time when that basketball player came in here and offered me $500 to fuck his brains out?" asked Mt. Everchest.

"Nah uh, tell us," said Cherry.

As Flower began changing clothes, she too sat down to listen.

"Let me tell you, the brother plays for the Knicks or something. So anyway, he offers me $500 to fuck his brains out so all I'm thinking is Chi-Ching! Jackpot! But see coming from out of West Virginia, no one ever told me how the brothers were hanging in their pants."

"Girl, you better recognize," said Cherry twisting up her face.

"Anyway, we go up in one of the V.I.P. booths and dude pulls out five $100 bills and hands them to me. So now I'm thinking, wow, how can I get him to become one of my regulars? I figure, I'm big, my big ass titties jingling all in his face while he's fucking me, me giving him my southern moan all at the same time, might get his rich ass open. He was a handsome fella too. So I pull my G-string to the side and I say, '*Come on big daddy*!' Before he pulls out his thing he says to me, 'Aye, big momma, do you know what it feels like to be pregnant 200 times?' So me being from the Midwest, I'm like duh. Girl, don't you know he pulls out this big ol' thang that looked like a young child's leg and says, 'Fucking with baby Anaconda, you're about to find out!' Don't you know that mothafucka shoved that thing up in me so far that I almost choked, if y'all get my drift," she said smiling. "Then that mothafucka stroked away for two hours straight. On that Ecstacy or off that Viagra shit. Every pump felt like a baby was in my stomach."

"What ever happened to him?" asked Cinnamon, mesmerized by the story, coochie wetter than a porno chick in heat.

"Girl, ol' boy pays me a personal visit at the crib every time they play at the Garden. And I still don't know his name. To top it all off, he get it all on the house," says Everchest making all of the ladies laugh.

"Aye youngin," said Cherry to Flower, who's now in a thong and matching bra.

"Yeah, what's up?" replied Flower, standing her ground.

"You new here?"

"Yup."

"Do you know what you're doing?"

She crossed her arms. "Basically."

"It ain't shit to wiggle your waist and shake your little ass baby girl, you just have to know how to tease."

A red light went off in the dressing room indicating that the stage girls are about to perform.

"Let's go y'all. Aye youngin, what's your name?" continued Cherry.

"Flower."

"Flower? Is that your stage name?"

"No, that's my real name."

"You need a stage name girl. Have some clown hunting you down and finding out where you live using your real name. Let me see," said Cherry looking her up and down. "Angel. Yeah, Angel."

"Why you call her Angel?" asked Cinnamon.

"'Cause, look at her, she's perfect. She ain't got no stretch marks, she got a nice apple ass. A nice chest. A gorgeous face. Beautiful natural hair. Ain't shit wrong with her. She has to be an Angel."

"Keep it girl," said Mt. Everchest, brushing past them.

"Let's go y'all," said Cherry.

"Come on," said Cinnamon.

All the girls rushed upstairs with Flower in tow. Flower thought to herself, "If only they knew."

Upstairs, the place was jamming. Music blasting, beautiful women everywhere and the men with the biggest bankrolls in the city were in the house. Center stage, club owner Tony Ciocca grabbed hold of the microphone as the DJ lowered the music.

"Good evening ladies and gentlemen. I'd like to welcome you to another night of Very Important People. I hope everyone has at least two drinks in their system by now. Please, I need the money," said Tony, causing a tidal wave of laughter.

"Well, we have a great show lined up for everyone this evening. We have three features and one local coming up here to give you guys a show like you've never seen before. Put your hands together because coming to this stage, from New York City, we have the very talented and very beautiful Mary J Thighs!"

The club shook from the applause. Mary J. Thighs, a 5'6" goddess with huge firm thighs, rode the stage like a jockey at the racetrack for three songs. Exiting the stage, she picked up all of her tips and retreated to a V.I.P booth with a customer who placed three $100 bills in her butt cheeks and whispered something into her ear.

Back to the microphone, Tony Ciocca dismissed Mary J. with a few jokes and introduced the next feature dancer.

"Bring your hands together, and give a warm welcome to this next young lady that's coming to the stage. All the way from Las Vegas, Nevada, we bring to you the fabulous, the extraordinaire, Britney Sphere's! Ladies and gentlemen, Britney gives new meaning to the term beautiful."

Britney, a gorgeous blonde with a perfect set of double D's, mimics three of pop artist Britney Spears' songs, all while never standing on her feet. Britney slid across the stage allowing every potential customer at arms reach get an up close and personal of her precious assets. After three songs, she too retreated to a booth with a lucky guy who either trades on Wall Street, or owns it.

Flower's Bed

Returning to the stage for a third time, Tony Ciocca introduced yet another gorgeous doll.

"Fellas, I know the first two women were out of this world. And fortunately, it doesn't stop there. So for all of you guys who like the exquisite, and love the exotic, without further ado, I bring to you the sexy, delicious, Conneee Thooong!"

All the lights in the club went dark and the music stopped. A single light pointed at the stage unveiling one of the most beautiful Asian women in the world. As the first song escaped through the speakers, Ms. Thong maneuvered her body into all sorts of acrobatic positions, mystifying the crowd and causing them to gasp at times. As Connee continued on, Flower walked over to Tony, who was now posted up near the DJ booth and asked him, "Can I go up there?"

"Up where?" he replied.

"Up there," said Flower pointing at the marvelous stage.

"You're Flower, J.R.'s friend, right?"

"Yes."

"Where is he? He hasn't been by in a few days?" said Tony.

"I think he's taking some time out to be by himself for a while. You know, recollecting, evaluating wrong moves, etc," said Flower forcing a smile.

"Yeah, I got you. Listen kid, today's your lucky day. Our local been on the shitter for the last half hour with the runs. And we don't need any mud baths going on, if you know what I mean. So have you ever stage danced before?"

"Yeah, in school. At talent shows and stuff."

"Well this ain't The Wizard of Oz and that stage there ain't the Yellow Brick Road. Connee here is on her last song, you got two minutes to give me your stage name and the names of your three favorite songs."

"Introduce me as Angel and play Doo Doo Brown by Luke. After that, tell the DJ he can play whatever he wants to play."

"Okay kiddo, get ready, you're almost up," said Tony heading toward the stage.

After dismissing Connee, Tony introduced Flower to the anxious audience.

"Ladies and gentlemen, I hope you're not worn out because it's time for our final act of the night. Tonight I'm going to bring to you a brand new era of dance. An era that is predicted to grow to unimaginable heights, like most of you men have been doing all night," said Tony, once again sharing his sense of humor.

The crowd laughed.

"Ladies and gentlemen, the V.I.P. Club presents the one, the only, Aaanngeell! And she truly is a blessing from God."

"Don't Stop Get It, Get It, Pop That Coochie Doo Doo Brown!" Those were the words that blared through the club's speakers as Flower walked the entire stage making her butt cheeks clap, shake, rattle and roll. The DJ never changed the song and Flower never stopped shaking her booty. She also never removed her top or bottom. At the end of her performance, Flower gathered up all of the money that was thrown on the stage or that fell from her waistband from her shaking so hard. She then retreated back to the dressing room to regain her composure.

"Girl, you are the bomb!" said Mary J. Thighs.

"You did your thing!" said Connee, in her Asian accent.

"Honey, you need to show us how you learned to back that thing up like that. I know you cleaned up Sugar. Take a break girl. Count up all of your money and put it somewhere safe. If you collected over $500, you might as well rest for the evening. Anything less than that, your ass better work those booths," said Britney.

The girls retreated upstairs to once again work the booths and hope to get lucky. Flower unballed all of the crumpled up bills and counted it up three times. She thought to herself, "$2,700. Oh shit! Jackpot!" She figured, "Fuck the booths for tonight. Cherry said I have to know how to tease. That was my teaser. That'll be my trademark from now on. Never get completely nude and never ever fuck with the booths."

"Angel! Angel!" shouted Cherry.

"Yo!" replied Flower.

"Good job youngin," said Cherry, peeking from the stairs that lead to the main floor. "Are you coming back up?"

"Nah, I think I'm going to chill out tonight. You know, just give them a teaser."

"You learn fast youngin. Keep up the good work." Then Cherry disappeared back into the club's atmosphere.

Flower was satisfied with her evening's earnings. She got dressed and caught a ride home with one of the bouncers. She snuck back into her apartment without waking up her mother and slid quietly into her bedroom. She picked up the phone and called Rosalyn.

Ring! Ring! Ring! Ring! Ring!

"Hello," said Rosalyn half asleep.

"Bitch, wake up," said Flower whispering.

"Damn ho, you always holla at me like I'm a booty call or something. What's up, are you okay?"

"Yeah I'm okay girl. I was at that club tonight."

"What! You danced?" said Rosalyn looking at her clock.

"Yeah."

"Did you make any money?"

"Almost three G's girl!"

"What? Three thousand? How many niggas you fucked?"

"I didn't fuck anybody. What the hell do I look like to you?"

"A ho."

"Yeah, whatever."

"How many dicks did you have to suck then?"

"Bitch, stop playing. None."

"Well, what did you do to make three thousand dollars?"

"I said almost three thousand dollars. And all I did was dance. I gave it to them ghetto style."

"For real?"

"Yup. That's all."

"Listen Flow, I'm tired as shit. Why don't we hook up tomorrow at school."

"Alright."

"Are you going to have the strength to wake up?" asked Rosalyn.

"I should, but if not, wake me up."

"Okay."

"Night Ros."

"Night Flow. Sweet dreams."

"I hope so."

Click.

CHAPTER EIGHT

The Metropolitan Detention Center, Downtown Brooklyn

7 a.m.

"Ayo son, who has that phone after you?" asked J.R. inquiring to another inmate about the cell block telephone.

"You son," replied the inmate.

J.R. waited patiently at the rear of the cell block until the telephone became available for usage.

"Ayo Black," shouted the inmate, hanging up the telephone and calling out to J.R.

J.R. acknowledged the guy by holding his hands up in the air and responding with a simple, "Yo!"

"Do you still want the phone?"

"Yeah, yeah. No doubt."

J.R. picked up the telephone and dialed 1-800-577-8478.

Ring! Ring! Ring! Ring!

"Hello, Crime Stoppers, may I help you?" said a dispatcher.

"Yeah uh, do I have to leave my name?" asked J.R.

"No sir, you may remain anonymous if you'd like. However, you will be referred by a number for future references."

"Alright, what if I knew something about something, could you like, help me?"

"I don't understand sir. You'll have to be more specific."

"Alright, listen, I'm in jail right."

"Excuse me?"

"I'm in jail, what?"

"Sir, are you trying to report a crime that occurred in prison?"

"No ma'am. I know something about a crime that happened in the streets."

"And you'd like to report it now that you're in jail?"

"Yes ma'am."

"Tell me sir, when did this crime take place?"

"First you have to tell me if you'll be able to help me."

"You mean, if you tell me what you know about a particular crime, I help you get out of your current situation?"

"That's exactly what I mean."

"Well sir, I have some good news and some bad news for you."

"Give me the bad news first."

"The bad news is, I can't help you. A District Attorney can."

"And the good news?"

"I can connect you with any prosecutor's office in the country. Would you like me to do that for you sir?"

"Yes ma'am."

"Sir, what state are you calling from?"

"I'm calling from New York."

"The city or the state?"

"I'm in New York City, Brooklyn, but the crime happened in the Bronx."

"That means you'll need to be connected with the Bronx District Attorney's office. Hold on please."

Transferring ...

Beep! Beep! Beep! Beep! Beep! Beep!

"District Attorney's office, Bronx County Floyd Murry speaking, may I help you?"

"Yeah uh, I was just on the phone with a lady from Crime Stoppers and she connected me to your office."

"Okay, and what can we do for you?" said Floyd tapping his pencil on a stack of papers.

"First of all, may I remain anonymous until I feel that I'm safe?"

"Sure you can. Just don't bullshit us. We have a lot of that you know."

"Do you have a number that I can call you back at because this phone is about to hang up?"

"Are you in jail sir?"

"Yes sir."

"Bronx House, Riker's Island, where?"

"I'm in MDC, Brooklyn."

"Oh, the Feds, I see. And you're sure that it is our office that you'd like to be dealing with?"

"Yes sir."

"Does your attorney know about this phone call?"

"Not yet."

"Are you going to notify him or her about it?"

"If I have to I will."

"Alright, hang your phone up and call us back in thirty minutes at 718-555-5556."

"It might be collect."

"It doesn't matter."

"Alright, bye."

Click! The line went dead.

The Bronx District Attorney's Office, 161st Street & Sheridan Avenue …

"Murry, did you get that?" asked Assistant District Attorney John Schnider.

"Just a second," replied Floyd Murry, Chief State Investigator.

"Coming, coming, coming! Here we go," added Murry, pulling out an entire rap sheet on J.R. from his printer after systematically tracing the call.

"He's Mr. Javon Richardson, identification number 64565-053. Instant offense, Capital Murder, Conspiracy to Commit Murder, Conspiracy to Distribute over 1 kilo of Cocaine Base and Money Laundering. Federal!" added Murry.

"Uh oh."

"Do you think that we have something here?" asked Murry.

"Maybe, I don't know," said Floyd removing his reading glasses.

"He also has a sheet for the state as well."

"Any of our people prosecute?" asked Schnider.

"Yeah, but we lost them all." Floyd rubbed the brim of his nose.

"Who'd he have, Johnny Cochran?" asked Schnider jokingly.

Looking at the rap sheet, Floyd said, "I don't know, but he sounds interesting."

"Get him back on the phone."

"You want me to call the jail?"

"You've done it before." Schnider gave his partner a look that said, "Don't act surprised now."

"But it'll seem like we're the ones soliciting."

"He called us, remember."

"You're right."

Dialing the number, Floyd Murry contacted the Metropolitan Detention Center in downtown Brooklyn.

"Hello," said a correctional officer.

"Yeah, uh, this is Floyd Murry of the Bronx District Attorney's office. I'm trying to locate and speak to if I can an inmate at your facility by the name, hold on a second," said Murry scrambling for the paper with J.R.'s name on it. "Javon Richardson."

"Do you have an identification number to go with that name, Mr. Murry?"

"Yes ma'am, 6-4-5-6-5-0-5-3."

"One second," said correction officer Grant, punching Mr. Richardson's identification numbers into her computer.

"He's on the 8th floor, unit three, 58 upper. His case manager is a Mr. Brian Gene."

"Can you connect me with Mr. Gene ma'am?"

"Yeah, hold on," she said pressing three numbers on her phone and then hanging it up.

Waiting ….

"Case manager's office, Mr. Gene here," said J.R.'s case manager answering his phone.

"Mr. Gene, this is Floyd Murry from the Bronx District Attorney's Office. An inmate on your case load contacted us not too long ago, but we were disconnected. We'd like to know if we could speak with him again at your convenience. His name is Javon Richardson."

"Sure, hold on," said Mr. Gene familiar with the name.

Over the intercom, Mr. Gene paged J.R.

"Javon Richardson! Javon Richardson! Report to your case manager's office."

"Mr. Murry, he should be up here in one second."

Holding the mouthpiece on the phone, Murry looked over at Schnider and whispered, "Piece of cake."

J.R. walked to his case manager's office and tapped on the window of the door.

Tap. Tap. Tap.

"Excuse me, sir, I'm Mr. Richardson. Javon. You called me over the speaker," he added.

"You have a phone call," said Mr. Gene handing J.R. the phone.

Giving his case manager a bewildered look, J.R. said to himself, "Who the fuck is on the phone for me?"

"Hello," said J.R.

"Mr. Richardson. How are you?" said Mr. Murry.

"Who am I speaking to?" asked J.R.

"I'm sorry, didn't you just call us about some information regarding a crime of some sort?"

"Oh shit, how'd you know it was me? Ayo, how did y'all find me?"

"That doesn't matter, Mr. Richardson. What matters is the information that you have for us. I know murder is serious. Especially with the Feds. You do know about their 95% conviction rate right?"

"So what, can y'all help me?"

"It depends."

"On what?"

"On what information you have for us."

J.R. remained silent for a few moments. Then he spoke up. "When can we meet?" asked J.R.

"Whenever you want to."

"Well let me call my attorney first and I'll have her call you guys with a date and a time."

"Suit yourself, Javon. Let's just hope it's something good. 'Cause murder is serious. You'll need to be able to offer something big before anyone even considers dealing with someone like you."

"What I have is big. Don't worry. In fact, you've wanted this information for some time now. I see promotions for your office."

"Alright Sammy, we'll talk with you at the meeting," said Murry referring to the Notorious Sammy the Bull, John Gotti's famous snitch.

"Okay, my attorney will contact you guys."

"Okay."

"Ah-ight, bye."

"Bye, bye."

Click.

"Thank you Mr. Gene," said J.R. hanging up the phone.

"Is everything alright?" asked Mr. Gene.

"Yes, everything is fine," said J.R. leaving his office.

"You think we got something?" asked Schnider.

"I hope so," said Murry. "I hope so."

CHAPTER NINE

Preparing for school, Rosalyn ironed her designer jeans and top and laid out a pair of ankle cut socks also known as boodies that matched her outfit. Since Rosalyn is an only child and her mother is off to work at 5 a.m. every day, she often strolls around her apartment in the nude until it's time to leave for school.

Tap. Tap. Tap.

"Who the hell is knocking at my door this early in the damn morning?" said Rosalyn, questioning herself aloud. "I know Flower's ass didn't leave the house before me this morning after last night's episode," she continued.

"Who is it?" Screamed Rosalyn, heading for the peephole on her front door.

"It's me, Rah," answered her boyfriend.

Unlocking and opening the door, Rosalyn asked, "What are you doing here Boo?"

"I came to holla at my baby. You have a problem with that?" asked Raheem, entering the apartment and following Rosalyn into her bedroom. "And where the hell are your clothes, sexy?" he added.

"Nigga, I just got out of the shower. My clothes are right here on my bed."

"Are you down for a quickie?" asked Raheem, with a smile that Rosalyn always found attractive.

She blushed. "You want to?"

"I guess you must've forgotten that guys get horny even when air hits us."

Moving her clothes from the bed to a chair, Rosalyn laid back on her elbows and invited Raheem to come join her. Removing all of his clothes except for his T-shirt and socks, Raheem climbed into the bed with Rosalyn and went face first toward her vagina. He licked and sucked and licked her again over and over until her vaginal lips were as moist as the lips on her face.

"Oooh! Oooh! Oooh! Oooh! Oooh! Oooh! Yes! Right there!" said Rosalyn moaning softly while pulling Raheem's head as close to her vagina as she could.

"Turn over," said Raheem softly.

"Wait, keep going Boo."

"Just turn over."

Rosalyn turned over and felt Raheem putting her in the doggystyle position. He then continued licking her, exploring her inner most folds. From asshole to clit, back and forth he went with his tongue until Rosalyn's bed sheets became a dripping pan. Raheem reached into his pants and pulled out a small packet.

"What's that?" asked Rosalyn, looking over her shoulder.

"Nothing," he said, ripping off a corner of the packet.

She chuckled, "You're doing something."

Licking her, Raheem concentrated on her clitoris while his hand lubed her anus.

She jumped. "What's that Raheem?"

"K-Y Jelly, why?"

"What are you up to?" she asked as she got back into her doggy style position.

"Nothing. Hold up," said Raheem as he positioned himself behind her and slid his member into her vagina.

Pumping in and out of her at a comfortable pace, Raheem began sticking his thumb in and out of Rosalyn's asshole matching the rhythm of their love making. After a few minutes, Raheem pulled out and said, "Lay flat on your stomach."

Complying, Rosalyn grabbed her pillow and buried her face into it. Raheem slowly slid his member halfway into Rosalyn's anus and stopped.

"Are you okay Boo?" he asked.

"Um hmm. Just go slow," said Rosalyn, keeping her head buried into the pillow.

Raheem repeated his half stroke method until he felt he could take it to the hilt.

"Deeper," she said.

Pumping harder, Raheem increased his speed and met Rosalyn's every hump.

"Mmmph! Mmmph! Mmmph!" moaned Raheem.

"Oooh yeah, this shit feels so good," he continued.

"Boom! Boom! Boom! Boom!

The banging on her front door startled both Rosalyn and Raheem. Stopping at full hilt, Raheem told Rosalyn to ask who was at her door.

"Who is it?" she screamed.

"Me, Flow."

"Ah damn. What the fuck. Is this bitch up selling newspapers or something?" asked Raheem angrily. "Damn!" he continued.

"Hold on," screamed Roslyn. "Hurry up," she whispered to Raheem.

Raheem began pumping in and out of her like a dude just coming from prison after doing ten years. Feeling his orgasm approaching, Raheem grabbed Rosalyn's shoulders and rammed her fast and hard until he released everything he had into her rectum.

"Oooh shit! Aahh!" he gasped.

Boom! Boom! Boom!

"Bitch hurry up. I have to pee," said Flower.

"Give me a second!" screamed Rosalyn.

Raheem got up and grabbed his clothes.

"I'm going to the bathroom yo," said Raheem.

Putting on her robe, Rosalyn opened the door for Flower.

"Damn bitch, you treat me like I'm a Jehovah's Witness or something," said Flower storming into the apartment.

"Ssshhh! Raheem is here," said Rosalyn putting her finger next to her lips.

"Where is he at?" whispered Flower.

"He's in the bathroom."

Flower twisted up her face. "What is he doing, taking a dump?"

"No stupid. That nigga just tore me a new asshole," said Rosalyn clutching her own butt cheeks.

"Girl, you let him go down the dirt road? Oooh." She covered her mouth.

"Shut up. My ass is killing me."

"You're a Power Ranger now."

"What the hell is a Power Ranger?"

"A bitch who takes it up the ass."

"Where did you hear that one at?"

"This nigga I was fucking with from Manhattanville Projects on 130th Street and Broadway."

"You let him do you in the butt Flow?"

"Hell no, but his ass thought he was slick and tried to tell me all these stories about bitches he fucked in the ass hoping that I'd become a Power Ranger myself."

"So you've never been fudge packed?"

"Hell no!"

"Excuse me, aren't you going to be late for something?" said Raheem walking into the living room fully clothed.

"Oh yeah, let me get dressed girl, give me a minute," said Rosalyn retreating back to her bedroom.

"Don't you like have cars to chase or something?" said Raheem.

"Fuck you nigga! I wish Alize was still here."

"And what the fuck was he going to do if he was still here?" said Raheem all up in Flower's face.

"Beat your motherfucking ass, bitch!"

"Flow. You know what? If your pops hadn't died, you might've turned out to be somebody." He turned and walked.

"Nigga I am somebody! Fuck you! Aye Ros, I'll meet you outside. I don't like clowns," said Flower leaving out of the apartment.

"Why are y'all two always fighting? Just ignore her," said Rosalyn to Raheem.

"Fuck her," said Raheem waving his hand.

"Raheem, don't talk like that about her, please."

"Okay Boo, only for you though." He kissed her on the cheek.

"Only for me then," said Rosalyn locking the door behind them.

"So I'll see you when you get home Ros."

"Okay Rah, I'll see you later," said Rosalyn taking the steps downstairs to the lobby.

The girls met in front of the building and headed toward Webster Avenue to catch the bus for school. On the ride there, Flower told Rosalyn about her first night working at the V.I.P. Club. Excited about the money she made, Flower promised Rosalyn she'd take her shopping to celebrate her new career.

At the entrance of the school, the girls prepared themselves for entering the school by pulling out their identification cards which must get swiped through an attendance machine at the school's lobby doors. When the students swipe their cards, small messages appear on a computer screen attached to the machine notifying the students of any appointments they may have or it simply tells them, "Good morning."

"Flow, where'd you get that from?" asked Rosalyn, pointing at something in Flower's pocketbook.

"What, this?" said Flower pulling out a Gucci keychain pouch.

"Yeah."

"I picked this up when I was over J.R.'s house."

"And you just kept it?"

"Hell yeah! It was cute, and besides, he could buy himself another one anytime."

"Are those all of your keys?"

"No, only one of them is mine. The rest I believe are his. I never removed any of his keys because it makes me feel like I own a lot of shit when I unlock my door. When people hear all of these keys jingling, they look at me and see the Benz key and all, and they think that I'm a baller."

"Girl, you're crazy!"

Bliiing! Bliiing! Bliiing! Class has begun …

"Uh oh, time to get in school," said Rosalyn.

The girls swiped their cards and Rosalyn's message read, "Good morning Rosalyn Harrison." It read the day, the date and the time and told her to have a nice day. When Flower swiped her card, it said, "Good morning Flower Abrams." It too gave her the day, the date and the time and it also told her to be at the guidance office for study period.

"Flower, why didn't your card light up the green light telling you to keep it moving? It lit up the blue light indicating that you had a message. Let me find out that you're making moves without your girl."

"I have to be at the guidance office during study period again. I guess Mrs. Berkowitz wants to see me."

"Did she diagnose you with anything yet?"

The duo walked side by side as they chatted away.

"I don't have anything. My mom was just worried about the nightmares I was having."

"Nightmares, you be having bad dreams Flow?"

"Sometimes, not everyday though."

"Are they scary?"

"A little bit. They seem more realistic than anything and that's the scary part."

"What do they be about?" asked Rosalyn, being persistent.

Bliiing! Bliiing! Bliiing! Movement is over …

"Ros, I'll talk to you at lunchtime."

"Okay Flow."

During the study period, Flower met up with Mrs. Berkowitz for another session. Greeting one another, the ladies got right down to business.

"Flower, I'd like to talk about something today that may not be an issue with you, but I see how those young fella's drool and ogle at you and I feel it's important that I share this information with you. Just for information purposes. So please, be open minded and bear with me. Okay?"

"Okay, Mrs. Berkowitz."

"Flower, I'd like to talk to you about rape and date rapes because a lot of times, it can happen to young women like yourself."

"What made you decide to talk about this topic Mrs. Berkowitz? I thought our main purpose was to help me deal with my father's death?" asked flower.

"It is, and I do, but I kind of sort of threw a few ideas around in my head that I felt may break the ice between us. I didn't think that using and abusing drugs would be a good topic today especially since your mom expressed to me how much you hate it when she drinks and how you use to hate it when Raymond smoked. So I eliminated that. I also eliminated the thought of you being a truant because you're at school almost all of the time. It's just that many of the girls that I've sat down and spoke with have gone through something like rape or date rape directly or through sharing it with someone that they know. But if you don't want to talk about it, we don't have to. In fact, here's what I'd like for you to do. Take these pamphlets here and read them," said Mrs. Berkowitz handing Flower some pamphlets on rape. "This way you'll be a bit more educated in that area in case you do come across a situation like that personally or otherwise. It'll prepare you to talk to people in a helpful manner and not seem so ignorant to that heinous crime. So here, keep those," said Mrs. Berkowitz pointing at the pamphlets that she gave Flower. "And go over them. And if you have any questions about any of it, please feel free to come and ask me anything, anytime, okay sweetie?" she smiled.

"Okay Mrs. Berkowitz. I will," said Flower leaving the guidance office.

Walking to catch the rest of her study class, Flower decided to read one of the pamphlets. It was titled "Rape: **Was It My Fault**?"

"Was it my fault?" was a question that Flower learned incredibly are the most common words uttered by rape victims after they have gone through that humiliating, degrading and violent intrusion. She also learned that 12.1 million American women who have been raped, the guilt, which occurs after the shock of that heinous event, is a natural part of the trauma of rape due to a series of events. One being the victim has been violated both physically and psychologically; often beaten, assaulted and threatened with death. Another being if she reports the rape, then she must face the harrowing experience of being examined by doctors and nurses, while facing the intense questioning of the police. To top it all off, there is also the fear of rejection by current or future intimate partners.

Unfortunately, the result of these horrible and stressful situations leaves many rape victims in a state of shock, anxiety, depression, flashbacks, nightmares and rage. Finally, the emotions and feelings of helplessness and a shattered self esteem will have her begin to wonder whether she could have done anything to avoid the painful, embarrassing and surrealistic situation in which she has found herself. If she doesn't report the rape, then she is left to her own damaged physical and psychological state in which she will eventually begin to point the finger at herself.

"Flow," said Rosalyn startling her. "What are you reading?" she asked.

"Nothing," said Flower, tucking the pamphlets into her book bag.

"So, how'd the session go this time around with Dr. Huxtable?"

"It's Berkowitz, and it was cool. It was informative. Are you ready to go to lunch now?"

"Yeah, let's go."

The duo headed to lunch and ended up spending the rest of the day together. Flower, still tired from the night before, decided to take it in early tonight. Tucking herself into bed and turning on the radio, Flower drifted off to sleep listening to the rhythmic melodies of the latest Hip Hop and R&B. But one question kept popping into her mind, "Was it my fault?" That's something she vowed to find out.

CHAPTER TEN

The V.I.P. Club …

"Angel, did you clean up the other night?" asked Mt. Everchest, "because guys were asking me about you the entire night," she added.

"A little something, not much though. Just enough to satisfy me, you know," said Flower changing into her dance costume.

"You should've stayed and tended to the booths. That's how you get your regulars and that's where the big money comes in at."

"Really?"

"Yeah. When I first came here, I strutted my stuff on that very stage and made close to four thousand dollars. I thought I had it made. I said, 'Shiiit, is this all I have to do? Ride this stage every evening like I'm at a rodeo and I'll make $4,000 doing it.' The next night I only made sixty dollars on the stage. I later found out that those men were giving me large amounts of money because they liked what they saw and hoped to get this fresh meat into one of the booths. I was just so nervous that first evening that I never looked at any of the customer's faces when they were putting money into my G-string. I was one of the lucky ones though, I learned quick. This other girl named Ivory that worked here gave me the game. She was white too, real petite though, and beautiful. All the guys loved her."

"Where's Ivory now?"

"After working here for about nine months, she left when she got her big break meeting some elderly millionaire guy in one of the booths about a year ago. They've been living happily ever after ever since."

"Do you ever speak with Ivory now?"

"Every once and a while. I think she's waiting for him to croak so she could inherit his fortune," said Mt. Everchest smiling.

"So what now?"

"Well, now I definitely pay more attention to the customers because many of them, whether you know it or not, simply want conversation."

"What, they just want to sit there and talk?"

"Yup! You see most of the guys that come here are married men and are having problems at home. Many of them really love their wives but their sex lives might be the problem. Like almost non-existent sometimes. So though they come here for sexual gratification, many of them achieve that satisfaction simply by talking to someone who'll listen."

"How often do you actually have sex with the customers?"

"I have sex with my basketball player. I call him King Tut. And every once and a while, if I'm horny and I want intercourse, I'll have it with one of the customers. But most guys are intimidated by my size and assume since I'm a dancer, I fuck all the time and they assume they won't be able to handle all of me. I'm fine with it though. I just rub on them with my ass or my hands for about ten minutes, and when they cum in their pants, I hand them some napkins, pick my money up and roll out."

"Do you think I can handle that Eve?"

"I think so mama. There isn't much to it. You set your own limits, your own prices. You're a woman, just be sexy, make it seem like you're listening to them, keep a smile on your face when necessary and grind, grind, grind girl."

"Good looking out Eve, I appreciate it."

"No problem Angel. I know how it is. Just don't make a career out of this shit. After a while, this shit becomes addictive and you begin to think that this is all that you can do. Finish school girl. Get your degree in something. Get your money, get out and start your own shit up. Anything. Nail salon, hair salon. Design clothes, do something. I want to invest in something myself. I don't know what it is yet. I may open up a book store. You know all of us women love to read. Just remember Angel, strippers don't make a whole lot of money when they're fifty years old and their chest is hanging all the way down to their knees."

The red light came on indicating that there's money to be made upstairs.

"I'll see you upstairs Angel," said Mt. Everchest making her way upstairs.

Flower got herself together and hit the main floor looking for potential customers waiting to be serviced. Passing one booth, Flower noticed a fat white guy in a green three piece suit sweating profusely, waving a wad of one dollar bills.

"Hey bitch, you want to come and give me some of what you got?" asked the guy.

"Hell no!" said Flower as she frowned up her face and moved on to another booth. At another booth a few yards down, Flower noticed a beautiful white lady in her early forties, who appeared to be lost, powdering her nose.

"Excuse me ma'am, are you waiting for someone?" asked Flower.

"Yes darling, I'm already taken care of. My time to climb Mt.

Everchest is coming up shortly. Thank you anyway sweetheart. And by the way, I don't eat dark meat."

"Well excuse me!" said Flower heading for yet another booth.

"Ayo shorty!" shouted a guy in another booth.

Flower looked his way and the guy motioned for her to come on over.

"Shorty, what's your name?"

"Angel," said Flower approaching the booth.

"That's a pretty name Angel. So tell me, are you really an angel or are you a devil in disguise?" asked the guy.

"I could be whatever you want me to be, for the right price," she said smiling.

"Oh really!"

"Yes really!"

"Sounds like my type of party. Well listen up. Why don't you come on over here and let us use a few minutes to get to know one another," said the guy, who looked West Indian and perhaps in his mid-twenties.

Flower walked into the booth and took the twenty dollar bill that he had in his hand and sat on his lap.

"So what's your name cutie?" asked Flower, lying.

"I think I might change my name to cutie since everyone here calls me that. My name is Freaky and that's fo sheezy."

"Why do they call you Freaky?" asked Flower, getting into her lap dance.

"If you really want to find out why they call me Freaky," said the guy handing Flower a fifty dollar bill, "you need to close that curtain there to find out."

Flower closed the curtain and Freaky instructed Flower to stand up.

"Continue dancing Angel," said Freaky removing all of his clothes except for his shoes and his socks. Well endowed, Freaky squirted some Vaseline from a small packet that he kept inside his pocket at all times and applied it to the head of his stiff member. Flower continued dancing, thinking to herself, "I hope this nigga doesn't think he's going to put that big ol' thang anywhere near me." Freaky began stroking himself and speeding up his pace as he kept his eyes glued to Flower doing her sexy dance moves.

"Oh fuck, I'm cumming! I'm cumming! I'm cumming goddammit!" said Freaky, jerking himself with intense strokes. As his orgasm approached, Freaky aimed the head of his penis at his own face and ejaculated all that he had all over his own nose and mouth. Witnessing the sadistic behavior, Flower ran out of the booth with Freaky yelling at her, "I told you I was Freaky! Bitch!"

"Oh my God!" said Flower catching up with Cherry.

Cherry stopped. "Girl you look spooked. Are you okay?"

"Cherry, why didn't you all tell me that there were disgusting weirdos that come to this club?"

"Angel, this ain't St. Patrick's Cathedral. You should've known that there'd be some crazy mothafuckas running around in here. What maniac scared you anyway, because I know half of the perverts that come around this neck of the woods."

"Some black mothafucka named Freaky."

"Did that nasty ass nigga get butt naked on you and jerk off all on himself again?"

"Yeah, disgusting mothafucka. That's disgusting!"

"Girl he caught all of us with that crazy shit. First it freaked us out, now, we just go, get our money, let him jerk off on his nasty ass self, then we leave his stupid ass right there to wipe the shit up."

"Are there any straight guys in here? I done ran into a Benny Hill look alike, some ol' white bitch that said she don't eat dark meat, this Pee Wee Herman ass nigga, I can imagine how the next cat is going to be."

"Hope for the best girl, and prepare for the worse. But there are some straight niggas up in here. Most of them just be laid back in the cut. You have to look hard, cause bitches be on them," said Cherry spotting one of her regulars. A heavy set black guy who eats her out for hours at a time without taking a break. "Angel, I'll see you later, dinner is about to be served," she added.

Flower decided to sit back in an empty booth and watch the stage show, when a guy walked up to the booth and startled her.

"Excuse me ma'am."

"Yeah, what's up?" said Flower.

"Is this booth occupied?"

"You see me in it don't you?" Her face was frowned up like if a foul odor was present.

"Damn sweetheart, why a beautiful girl such as yourself have to be so mean? I just want a place to relax, that's all."

"My apologies, I'm in a fucked up mood right now. But don't mind me," said Flower rolling her eyes.

"Are you going to move your feet or are you going to let them sit here in my face?"

"Nigga I've been on my feet all day and they're killing me. So I'm going to sit my feet right where they are until I feel like moving them."

The stranger sat down, grabbed Flower's feet and placed them into his lap and began removing her pumps.

"Oh, another one," thought Flower to herself. "Except this one has a foot fetish. I guess he wants me to jerk him off with my feet."

However, Flower was surprised at what happened next. Before removing Flower's second shoe, the guy extended his hand out to her and said, "I'm sorry, I didn't formally introduce myself. My name is Shawn. And you are?"

"I'm Angel," said Flower responding to his hand shake.

Shawn began massaging Flower's feet causing her to instantly relax. Something she needed in light of all the drama that was going on in her life.

"Are you a masseuse or something?" asked Flower.

"No, I did take the course in high school though."

"What school did you attend?"

"I went to King, down in Manhattan, then I went out to Farmingdale, out on Long Island."

"Did you graduate?"

"No, I dropped out!"

"Why'd you drop out?"

"It's a long story."

"Well I have some time if you do."

"And how much is it going to cost me?" said Shawn stopping his massage.

Flower smiled. "It depends."

"Depends on what?"

"Depends on how long we sit here," said Flower smiling.

"I have to tell you, I only have about $300 on me. So once you feel that I've exceeded that amount, stop me!"

"Okay," said Flower laughing.

He leaned back and began telling his story. "Well I was born and raised in the Bronx."

"Where at?"

"River Park Towers."

"I know where that's at."

He looked at her. "You've been there before?"

"No, I just been around. I mean it's right off of the Major Deegan Expressway anyway. Continue, please."

"Anyway, after high school, I entered Farmingdale on a scholarship for Computer Engineering. My high school sweetheart and I moved into a nice little apartment we found off campus. Things were going good. I got my Associates when I was 19, and I wanted to keep it up until I got my Masters. My fiancée, however, was unfortunately diagnosed with type 1 lupus. It's like cancer. There are stages to it and unfortunately, my shorty was diagnosed with the most severe of the stages. Many people with lupus live long lives with proper medical care. Prescription drugs, therapy, we tried everything. She just wasn't strong enough. The disease ate her up. She was diagnosed, then six months later I'm making funeral arrangements. Her death tore me up. I was distraught for months. I ended up doing a complete 360 with my life. I quit school, I got on a short drinking binge and I got in trouble with the law over a fight I had at a bar. The arrest slowed me down a little bit. I got a job at an elite massage parlor out in the Hamptons and began an affair with one of the exclusive customers. A Columbian lady with an extremely rich cartel husband. Hey, let me know if I'm boring you," said Shawn pausing again.

"No, I'm listening. Actually I'm enjoying what I've heard so far. You're very interesting."

"Have I exceeded my $300 limit yet?"

Blushing, Flower told him that he hadn't yet.

"Continue," she said.

"So this Columbian lady realizes that our relationship is too dangerous for the both of us, so one day she drops by and leaves a package for me. I come by to pick it up and I read the note that is attached to it. It's telling me all this mess about how she's madly in love with me and yada yada this and yada yada that. So I get home and I open up the package and it's a key. A key to my new life."

"A key to your new life? Explain."

"Well, it was definitely literally a key. A key to a safety deposit box for which the contents inside brought me into a new life."

"Angel, we need you over here!" shouted Cinnamon.

"I'm busy Cinnamon. Can't you get one of the other girls?" asked Flower.

"No I can't get one of the other girls Angel, which is why I'm asking you." Cinnamon had her hands on her waist.

"Alright, give me one second."

"I'll be downstairs Angel," said Cinnamon. She walked off.

"Okay."

"It's all good, it's getting late anyway. So how much do I owe you?" asked Shawn.

Seeing Shawn in the light, Flower realized that he bore a striking resemblance to her father. Almost frightening.

"You know what, I have to go. Don't worry about it. This one was on the house," said Flower.

"No, it's not on the house. This is your job. This is what you get paid to do. Here," he said, placing the money into her hand instead of her panty line. "Take it. You take care of yourself Angel and be careful around here. I'll see you around," he added before disappearing into the club's atmosphere.

After helping Mt. Everchest find her car keys, all of the ladies noticed that it was getting late and they all decided to call it an evening.

"Angel, did you luck up tonight?" asked Mt. Everchest.

"I don't know Eve. I'm not sure."

"Oh well, tomorrow's another day."

"Yeah, tomorrow's another day," said Flower.

"Angel, do you need a ride home," asked Cherry.

"No, I'm okay. I'm going to take the bus home tonight. Need to relax a bit and think."

"Okay, peace out."

"Night y'all," said Flower.

"Bye," said all the girls at the same time.

Flower rode the bus home that evening allowing her mind the freedom it needed to wander. She began reminiscing about the good times she had with her father and the fun times that she had with Alize. A tear slowly crept from the lower part of her eye in remembrance of the two men she loved so dearly. She sniffled a couple of times, then shook it off. "I'll be okay," she thought, "I have no other choice but to be okay."

CHAPTER ELEVEN

The Interrogation Room at the Metropolitan Detention Center, Brooklyn …

"What do you think it is that our Mr. Richardson has for us?" asked Assistant District Attorney John Schnider.

"For what it's worth, I'm going to bet that the defendant is willing to make a deal to testify against his friends in Ohio," replied Chief Investigator Floyd Murry.

Tap! Tap! Tap! Tap!

Standing up, Floyd Murry told the people who were knocking to come in. Walking in were J.R. and his court-appointed attorney, Ms. Julia Meyers, a white lady, late twenties, blonde hair, green eyes with a petite build.

"Hello everyone," said Ms. Meyers.

"Hey, I'm John Schnider, prosecuting attorney, and this is my chief investigator, Floyd Murry," said Schnider introducing the two.

Everyone shook hands with the exception of J.R.

"Getting right down to business if you don't mind, I have filed a motion with the court regarding extradition and I also filed a motion for severance. I'd like my client's case prosecuted here in the southern district of New York and I'd like him tried separately from defendants Harold Dupont, Damion Henry and Jermaine Thompson," said Ms. Meyers referring to her paperwork.

"Ms. Meyers, I thought we were called down here because your client had some vital information for us," said Mr. Schnider.

"We do, I was just informing you of what you have in store in case you decide to decline our deal."

"Well let us hear what you have," said Schnider.

"First things first. The information my client is about to disclose to you involves a very serious case. Here are documents stating that if my client's information is not accepted by your agency for whatever reason, that your agency cannot act on the information or use the information unless you've obtained it on your own. And at this point, it's obvious that you are nowhere close to obtaining this information on your own. So would you please sign this Mr. Schnider?" said Ms. Meyers sliding the district attorney a copy of the documents.

After looking over the documents, Mr. Schnider signed them and silently prayed to himself that the information would be useful. Passing it back, Ms. Meyers glanced at the signature and told everyone that they were ready to begin.

Investigator Floyd Murry pulled out a small tape recorder, a legal pad and a pen. Looking over at J.R., Mr. Murry nodded his head looking for a response from the defendant to proceed.

"I'm ready Ms. Meyers," said J.R.

"You may start recording when you're ready Mr. Murry," said Ms. Meyers.

"Begin please," said Mr. Schnider looking at both Murry and J.R.

"On August 3, 1994, me …"

"State your full name for the record please, and your street name as well," said Murry briefly interrupting J.R.

"Okay. On August 3, 1994, me, I'm Mr. Javon Richardson, also known as J.R., and my friend," clearing his throat, he continued, "my old friend Tracy Barrow, also known as Alize, were in Columbus, Ohio at a B.P. gas station on Morse and Karl Roads. That's on Columbus' north side. Anyway, we met with three individuals there at or around 7:30 p.m. These individuals are now known as Harold Dupont, also known as Bear, Damion Henry, also known as Ness, and Jermaine Thompson, also known as B.G. At that time, I asked, decedent Tracy Barrow, what we were doing out there. He said, that some friends of his were going to meet him there because they owed him some money. So Jermaine, Damion and Harold pulled up in a dark colored two-door Regal and all exited the car. Tracy introduced all of the guys to me as Bear, being their superior, and Ness and B.G. as the enforcers. Then the four of them converged together and began having a conversation."

"Could you hear what they were saying Mr. Richardson?" asked Mr. Schnider.

"I could only hear a few words at a time."

"Could you tell us what those few words that you heard were."

"I heard something about 'Shoot him,' and 'Make sure he's dead,' and 'He's a bad person.' That was about all I was able to make out."

"Okay, continue Mr. Richardson."

"So the guys left and Tracy and myself drove back to the airport in a rental car and boarded a plane back to New York."

"Did you guys use your real names to purchase the tickets to fly back to New York?"

"No we didn't."

"Did you guys fly to Ohio from New York?"

"No sir, we drove. We drove the rental car there."

"Oh, I see."

"May I finish sir?"

"Sure, go right ahead."

"So like three days later, Tracy came to get me early in the morning from an acquaintance's house. Then we went back to his place on 169th Street where I saw the three Ohio guys again. So I asked him why are they here in New York and he told me that they were there to take care of some business for him. So I say cool. So we're sitting around just kicking it until around noontime and then the four of them exited the apartment and leave me in there all by myself. Tracy told me that he'd be back in about an hour or so, so I chilled. I waited there alone for about two hours. At maybe two o'clock, they all came back to the apartment sweating profusely and Tracy told me to come with them. So we all left and headed for the airport."

"Which airport?" asked Schnider.

"Laguardia."

"Continue."

"So after we dropped them off I asked Tracy, I call him by his street name though, I said, 'Alize, what's going on? What's popping?' Then he told me how they killed some people in a small grocery store on 211th Street and White Plains Road in the Bronx."

"Did he tell you why he killed these people?"

"No."

"Did he tell you who did the actual shootings?"

"Yeah."

"Mr. Richardson, would this be the case involving a Mr. Raymond

Abrams and three Hispanics?"

"Yes sir, that's definitely the same case."

"Did he tell you how everything went down Mr. Richardson?"

"Yes."

"Mr. Richardson, just out of curiosity, why would your friend tell you exactly what happened in that store? Why would he even tell you about it at all? I would think committing a crime as serious as quadruple homicide, that someone would keep that to themselves."

"You see, Alize bragged a lot. He always wanted people to think he was more than what he was when in reality, he was nothing but a punk."

The last remark J.R. made caused Murry and Schnider to wonder about something.

"Mr. Richardson, could you tell us how the incident took place according to what Mr. Barrow told you?" asked Murry.

"Yes sir. He said that they all went up in the spot and Bear shot the fake ass security guard off of a ladder or a stool that the guy used as a command post. That one shot killed the dude instantly. He didn't even move after that."

"How do you know that the man didn't move after that Javon?"

"Because Tracy told me. He bragged about everything. Every single thing. From how big his dick was to how much money he was making. Listen, I'm just telling you what he told me, but I'm using my imagination to give you guys a better perception of what happened. So anyway, after clapping dude off of the ladder, Bear and one of the other guys walked over to the counter and shot the other two store employees. Then Tracy said, 'Yo, let's clean out the cash register and make it seem like it was a robbery!' So they took the money out of the cash register, and in walked the target."

"The target?" said Schnider.

"Yeah, Raymond. Raymond was the intended target."

"Why the hell would Raymond be the intended target? Was he into something illegal?"

"I doubt it, but I know whatever it was, it was personal."

"So they shot all of these innocent people when in reality only one person was the target? I don't understand. I mean, why not just hit Raymond on the street when he was alone? Why risk getting caught doing something big like that?"

"Mr. Schnider, it's simple. It's the same reason why you guys never found who the killers were in the first place. You guys thought that a robbery had gone bad and that Raymond was in the wrong place at the wrong time. Right? Wrong! Raymond was in the perfect place at the perfect time. Had he been killed anywhere else, like on the street alone, you guys would've been digging deep into Raymond's business and probably would've found something to tie the murder to Tracy."

"Like what?"

"I don't know. Tracy knew it all. It was his plan, his reasons and his men who did it."

"Anything else Mr. Richardson?"

"No sir," said J.R. looking over at his attorney.

"Ms. Meyers, would you mind if you and your client left me and Murry here alone for a minute? We'd like to discuss some things," asked Mr. Schnider.

"No, go right ahead. We'll be in the next room discussing some things as well," said Ms. Meyers exiting the room with her client.

"Murry, are you thinking the same thing that I'm thinking?"

"You're damn right! This Richardson is a piece of shit who killed his friend more than likely over jealousy. I think he was there when Raymond got capped and I think he knows something else that we don't. We need to know why Raymond got murdered. Then we'll find out who pulled the trigger," said Schnider.

"Richardson's case with Barrow is federal. Isn't your brother-in-law still with the bureau?" asked Murry.

"Yeah."

Tap! Tap! Tap!

"Come in," said Murry.

Walking in, Ms. Meyers began to speak. "My client wants to know if you guys want to make that deal with the United States Attorney Michael Schwartz."

"Ms. Meyers, we have to give our superiors a full report which takes a day or two, so we'll have to get back to you on this as soon as possible," said Schnider.

"But are you interested?"

"Oh, yes ma'am. We're definitely interested. And so are the families of all those who died in that store. So please, let us get back to you on this one."

"Alright, contact my office as soon as your office is ready to deal."

"No problem Meyers," said Schnider as he escorted the woman to the door.

"Floyd, contact everyone that you know. Get as many people on this as you need. Immediately! I want airport records, rental car records, everything! I want you to check out that store again and make them remember whether or not their surveillance cameras were working that day. Find out if they were doing anything illegal! Also, talk to Raymond's family again. We need to know if Raymond was into anything in his neighborhood that dealt with Barrow. Get everything that you can on Barrow and Abrams! Get some people on Dupont, Henry and Thompson! Find out where they were July, August and September of '94! Find out ..."

"Whoa! Whoa! Whoa!" said Floyd. "John, didn't we just sign a form preventing us from pursuing this information?"

"No, Floyd, we signed a form preventing us from acting on Javon's information. We could still obtain information on our own because the case is still open. The investigation isn't over, it's just been stagnant for a while."

"So do you think Javon helped kill those people?" asked Floyd.

"I think Javon is a piece of shit and if he did kill those poor people, I want him to pay for it."

"Yeah, I hear ya. It's like ever since Sammy ratted on Gotti, everyone wants to make a deal now."

"That shit only works in the feds. We in the state want everyone to pay."

"Let's get on it then John."

"Come on Floyd."

CHAPTER TWELVE

Evander Childs High School …

"Flower, you're really beginning to enjoy being a stripper," said Rosalyn.

"It's paying the bills," said Flower.

"What bills? Your mama pays for everything. Besides, what do Mrs. Melinda say about you staying out late all the time?"

"Nothing, I just let her know that I'm alright, I let her know that I'm in school everyday and that I'm seeing Mrs. Berkowitz. My mom is cool. You know that already."

"Well is it scary working at that club around all of those weirdos?"

"It can get scary. I told you about the guy named Freaky right?"

"Yeah, the one who likes to shower himself with himself," said Rosalyn, causing the two of them to laugh. "So what's up with that one guy who poured out his personal life story to you? You said he was cute right?"

"Yeah, but I don't know Ros. I'm not really trying to get personal with any of the customers. He seemed nice and all, but then again, I don't even really know him like that. First of all, he's a customer. Secondly, we only kicked it for a couple of hours."

"That's the same guy that you said reminds you of your dad right?"

"Yeah, sort of. I guess he just resembles my dad a little bit in the face. I don't know."

"Are you going to see him again?"

"I don't know. I mean, if he comes back to the club, I'll sit and talk with him again. I have no problem with that."

"You better get yours girl," said Rosalyn laughing with Flower.

Bliiing! Bliiing! Bliiing! Bliiing!

"Flower, are you coming to study class or are you going to sit with Dr. Kavorkian again?"

"Shut up stupid! Mrs. Berkowitz is nice. You need to sit your Raheem loving ass down with somebody and talk about some things once in a while."

"I do, Raheem."

"I bet you do. But yeah, I'll be shacking up with Mrs. Berkowitz again. She helps me clear my mind you know. The club, my father, Alize, J.R., that shit can be stressful for a while."

"I can imagine. So I'll see you at lunchtime Flow."

"Okay."

"Holla!" said Rosalyn walking to her class.

Third period, The Guidance Office …

"Hello Mrs. Berkowitz, how are you doing this morning?" asked Flower.

"I'm fine Flower, thank you. And yourself?" asked Mrs. Berkowitz.

"I'm okay. I'm doing better actually." Flower took a seat.

"Really?"

"Yes, after talking with you and all, the last couple of times, I've been feeling a whole lot more at ease and I really appreciate you taking your personal time out to come and talk with me."

"It's nothing dear."

"Yes it is. In the beginning, I had doubts about this whole idea, but then we had our first conversation and you were so nice. I prejudged you and I shouldn't have. That's another thing that I learned dealing with you, patience. I have a lot more patience now and it's made my life a heck of a lot easier."

"Wow, that's wonderful. I am so proud of you Flower."

"Thank you."

"So, did you read the pamphlets that I gave you the other day?"

"I sure did."

"Care to discuss anything?"

"Sure, why not."

"Okay, you can begin when and where you like."

"Okay, Mrs. Berkowitz. Do you think victims of rape contribute to their own rape?"

"In my opinion and according to statistics, study shows that there are conflicted emotions of the spouses or partners of the rape victims, who in their despair and shock will also lash out and become angry with the victims; thinking they could have avoided the rape or somehow have done more to fight off the rapist. There are also many angry voices in society who make it more difficult for the victims by believing and loudly espousing that the victims often contribute to their own rape."

"Why would people do that Mrs. Berkowitz? Don't these people know that by doing that, victims will become discouraged?"

"Flower, many of these people have never been victims themselves or even know people who've been victimized. These are people who just went to school and are in it simply for the paycheck. They don't understand honey, and it's sad."

"Have you ever been a victim yourself Mrs. Berkowitz?"

"I'm glad that you asked that question Flower. But the answer is no, but I have counseled some who have been victimized."

"So what would make people believe that women want to get raped?"

"Well, some people believe that if you wear provocative or ultra-sexy clothing that means you're asking for it. Especially in today's fashion where skin is exposed."

"So people automatically assume since you're wearing a halter top and shorts that you want to be raped?"

"It's not only that Flower, it also has to do with the company one keeps. For example, certain clubs are notorious for date rape drugs being slipped into drinks and women being assaulted in the bathrooms. Yet those same clubs remain popular amongst you young kids. Also, placing oneself in unsafe environments or situations such as jogging in unpopulated areas or walking home alone, late at night, through isolated neighborhoods."

"I feel you totally Mrs. Berkowitz and now that I'm beginning to understand, I think I can agree with you. I also think being sexual with your date, you know, like engaging in heavy petting or making out for long periods of time can cause your partner to assume it's a green light for sex as well."

Bliiing! Bliiing! Bliing! Bliiing!

"Aw man," said Flower, upset that the ending of the period came of the session between her and Mrs. Berkowitz.

"I know," said Mrs. Berkowitz sympathizing with Flower. "I know what, here, take this," added Mrs. Berkowitz handing Flower another pamphlet.

"Steps A Woman Should Take If Raped," said Flower reading aloud.

"Read that carefully Flower and keep it somewhere safe because I've come across many young ladies who've messed up criminal cases against their assailants because they didn't know those steps. Okay?"

"Okay Mrs. Berkowitz. Thanks again. And I'll be sure to go over these steps. Bye now."

"Bye sweetie," said Mrs. Berkowitz smiling at Flower as she exited the guidance office.

Heading to her next class, Flower quickly read over the three steps a woman should take if raped. Number one was: Don't wash or douche. Because you do not want to wash away any evidence that could be used against your attacker in court. The second step was to notify the police and tell them everything that happened. And if you're afraid to notify the police, then call one of the many local rape crisis centers. The last step was to go to an emergency room for examination purposes and allow the doctor to make a record of the injuries and treat them. Samples of any fluid left in the vagina or anus, especially semen, will be gathered.

"Flow!" screamed Rosalyn.

"Yeah!" said Flower making her way through the crowd of students to get to Rosalyn.

"Girl how come every time you leave Mrs. Berkowitz' sessions, you're always on cloud nine?"

"Because, I'm often thinking about what she and I talked about."

"So is she helping you?"

"I think so."

"Just don't go 7:30 on me. You know, crazy and stuff."

"Trust me, I won't."

Bliiing! Bliiing! Bliing! Bliiing!

"Time to go girl. Are you coming to lunch?" asked Rosalyn.

"Hell yeah, I'm starving!"

"Let's go then."

"Let's go!"

And the two girls headed off to lunch, one thinking about food, and the other thinking about her father.

CHAPTER THIRTEEN

Back at Flower's apartment, she prepared herself for another night at the club. She stuffed three sets of matching thong underwear, a few cosmetics including makeup and hygiene products, and then she grabbed her keys.

"I wonder if these keys belong to J.R.'s apartment? First I need to find out if he still lives there," she thought to herself. "Let me call their directory," she continued.

Flower grabbed her cellular phone and dialed information.

Ring!

"Hello, Information, what city please?" asked the operator.

"New York City, the Bronx," said Flower.

"Hold please."

Beep! Beep! Beep! Beep!

"Information, may I help you?" asked an operator.

"Yes, um, may I have the phone number to the rental office for the Tracy Towers Apartment Complex?"

"One moment please," said the operator punching in digits on her computer. "Here it is," added the operator, transferring Flower to a computer message.

Flower's Bed

"The Rental Office hours at the Tracy Towers Apartment complex are from 7 a.m. to 4 p.m. Monday through Friday. Our main office phone number is 718-555-1873."

Click!

Flower wrote down the number as fast as the operator spit it out. Dialing it, she cleared her throat and prepared to change her voice.

"Hello, Tracy Towers," said a receptionist.

"Hi, my name is Joanne Richardson and I just drove down from Providence, Rhode Island. My brother is having a birthday party and he won't answer his phone. Can you tell me if his lobby number rings. You know, the number I'd dial if I were in the lobby trying to get in?"

"The lobby phone is hooked up to his direct phone line."

"Well could you please try him for me?"

"Sure I just need his name."

"It's Javon Richardson. J-A-V-O-N Richardson."

"Hold on ma'am."

Waiting, Flower kept her fingers crossed hoping the apartment wasn't registered to another name.

"Ms. Richardson."

"Yes ma'am."

"Your brother's line is just ringing."

"Oh okay. I'll try again when I pull up out front."

"Okay then."

"Bye, bye."

Click!

"I might as well check his place out. Hopefully I'll find something of good use," thought Flower to herself.

Ring! Ring! Ring! Ring!

"Hello," said Flower answering her cellular phone.

"Angel! Are you coming to work today?" asked Cinnamon.

"I'm on my way now Cin," replied Flower.

"Okay girl, 'cause it's bumping tonight. Plus you got a few of your customers here asking for you."

"Alright, I'll be there in a minute."

Click.

The V.I.P. Club

"Aye girl, what's up!" said Cherry.

"You girl! I see you're doing your thing!" said Flower referring to the money hanging from Cherry's underwear.

"Have you seen Cinnamon?" asked Flower.

"She's around here somewhere. Probably in one of the booths getting her freak on," replied Cherry. "Mt. Everchest was in booth six a little while ago as a matter of fact."

"Oh, I'm going to go and holla at her right now."

"Okay."

Walking over to booth six, Flower caught Mt. Everchest with her legs cocked behind her neck with a white woman's face glued to her love box. She could tell that Mt. Everchest was enjoying every minute of it by the way she was moaning and the facial expression she had on her face.

"Ah, ah, ah, ah, ah, ah, ah, ah, ah, ah, ah, ah!" moaned Mt. Everchest as the white woman shook her head from side to side while never removing her tongue from Mt. Everchest's clitoris. "Ah, ah, ah, ah, ah, ah, ah, ah, ah, ah, aaaaaahhhh!" she continued as she neared her orgasm.

Flower just stood there amazed.

Opening her eyes, Mt. Everchest noticed Flower staring at her. "Angel! Angel!" said Mt. Everchest snapping Flower out of her trance.

"Huh," said Flower.

"Give me a minute girl."

"Okay," said Flower walking over to an empty booth.

A few moments later, Mt. Everchest entered the booth where Flower was waiting.

"Angel, why you ain't working girl?"

"I'm about to do my thing in a minute. I just wanted to say hello to everyone, but I walked up and found you in a compromising position," said Flower laughing. "I guess everything is cool between the two of you now," she added.

"Girl, money is money."

"But you looked like you were enjoying it Eve."

"I was girl. Ain't nothing like a woman eating your pussy. She knows what to do because she'd want it done that way."

"So you're a lesbian?"

"If that's what you want to call it. I mean I'll basically do anything as long as the money is right. Shiiit, if a relative of mine want some of this and his or her money is right, heeeyy!" said Mt. Everchest laughing.

"Girl, you're crazy."

"That's that West Virginia shit coming up out of me."

"I heard that."

"Excuse me," said a voice from an adjacent booth.

Mt. Everchest peeked over to see who it was. "Angel, I think this one is for you."

"Who it is?"

"Come over here and see for yourself," said a familiar voice. Walking over, Flower noticed that it was the guy Shawn from the other night.

"Hi Shawn."

"Hey sexy, how are you?"

"I'm fine."

"Are you on the clock, or are you on a break?"

"I'm always on the clock."

"Well get on over here then!"

"What do you want, a lap dance?"

"I mean, do your thing. Stand in front of me and let me admire you for a minute."

Dancing for a couple of minutes, Flower earned herself two hundred dollars.

"What's this for?" she asked.

"It's for you Boo. I like the way you dance."

"But you gave me four fifty dollar bills and it's only been two minutes."

"Well you deserve it. I think you're worth it."

"Okay then, be my guest," said Flower as she continued dancing.

"Enough, enough," said Shawn becoming aroused.

"What! Let me do me!" said Flower really getting into her dance moves. Flower bounced up and down, shaking her hips and twisting her waist around and around until she figured Shawn was fully aroused again.

"Fuck it! Give me a lap dance!" said Shawn.

Flower jumped on him and began grinding like it was no tomorrow. She did so for four songs.

"Uh, uh, uh, uh, uh!" said Shawn reaching an orgasm.

Smiling, knowing that she had satisfied her customer, Flower passed Shawn some napkins and began to exit the booth.

"Hold on shorty. I'm going to go to the bathroom and clean myself up. When I come back, I want to kick it with you some more."

"Take your time lover boy, a girl needs to powder her nose too."

Flower and Shawn met back up in the booth about thirty minutes later and began chatting.

"So what's up?" asked Shawn.

"You cutie," said Flower.

"You think I'm a cutie?"

"Yeah, I think you're very handsome."

"You're very attractive yourself Angel."

"I see you're still at it girl," said Mt. Everchest walking by.

"That's right! Make money money, make money money money!" They said together laughing.

"So when are you gong to let me know a little bit about you?" asked Shawn.

"As soon as I learn more about you."

"What else is there to know about me?"

"Tell me why a handsome guy like yourself didn't reacquaint with anyone since your girlfriend died?"

"I tried dating, but it didn't work out because of the baggage that I was carrying. I needed to do something to get my mind off of everything. So after meeting the Columbian lady and given that key to my new life, I haven't had the time to get to know anyone because my life has been real hectic lately."

"You never did tell me what was in that safety deposit box. Would you mind sharing that with me now?"

"No, I don't mind. However, I'll feel uncomfortable telling you exactly what was in that box so how about you use your imagination and your common sense and read in between the lines. I'm basically a salesman, but I deal with people in the hood. And what I sell don't require a prescription."

"You don't have to say anymore. But tell me, why do so many guys seem to be in that type of business. Especially young black men?"

"Sometimes we try it out of curiosity and sometimes, whether you want to agree with me on this one or not, but, sometimes we do it because we have to."

"What do you mean by, you have to?"

"It's easy to explain, but it's going to be hard to understand. Put it this way. Going to college doesn't guarantee you a job when you graduate. It's just a reference and it looks good on your résumé. Now some people become discouraged and the only opportunity available at the time is the streets. You hear about so many people that somehow made it. They jumped in the game for a while, stacked some money, started their own business, then got out. Some people aren't so lucky."

"So what about you. Are you going to get what you need and then get out too?" asked Flower.

"That's my plan. I estimate it'll take about four more months and I should have what I need. Then I'm quitting for good."

"What are you going to do when you quit?"

"Buy some real estate. I figure people always need a place to live. As long as it's affordable. Plus I took two real estate classes at Farmingdale so I'm familiar with the field."

"At least you want to get your shit together. I know guys who've been on the corner for years and still don't have anything to show for it."

"I know a few like that myself."

"So what are you going to do, sit here and pay me all night to dance?" asked Flower.

"Why, you're trying to get out of here or something?"

"I don't care."

"Are you hungry?" asked Shawn.

"No, I just ate. I'm tired for real, for real."

"Do you want me to take you home?"

"I thought you were going to say your place. Most niggas don't need a woman to spell it out for them. Especially a stripper."

"First of all, I'm not most niggas. And you're not a stripper, you just work as one. And second of all, maybe I want more than just one night with you."

"Really?"

"Really!" said Shawn firmly.

"Let me get my things and I'll meet you out front."

"Ah-ight."

Flower took ten minutes to freshen up and change. Outside, she met Shawn as he pulled up in his late model Jaguar. "Get in Angel!"

"Is this your car?"

"Yeah."

"Just checking," said Flower smiling at Shawn.

Pulling up to the Esplanade Gardens Apartment Complex on 147th Street and Lenox Avenue in Harlem, Shawn drove his Jaguar into the building's underground garage. The duo reached Shawn's 26th floor apartment and were greeted by Shawn's puppy Rottweilers.

"Hey pups, what's up niggas!" said Shawn as the canines jumped and licked on him excitedly.

"How old are they?" asked Flower.

"They're four months old, tomorrow. I have the papers on them and all."

"What are their names?"

"The boy's name is Hypo, and his sister's name is Beserk. I know their names sound crazy, but these guys are really sweet animals."

"Come here little pups," said Flower bending down to pet the two dogs.

"Aye, why don't you make yourself comfortable while I clean their shit and refill their water and food bowls," said Shawn walking the dogs to the rear of his apartment.

Instead of doing her usual snooping, Flower simply admired the apartment noting that there were no purchases of any appliances that were too expensive to pronounce or unnecessary for use. He had beige wall-to-wall carpet, a black leather living room suit and a 26 inch color television set with two end tables. A Bose entertainment center sat opposite the entrance door with one side housing his two D.V.D. players while the other side housed his Super Nintendo video game system.

Reentering his living room, Shawn found Flower sound asleep on his sofa. He quietly retrieved a comforter from his linen closet and laid it over Flower without disturbing her peaceful sleep.

Early the next morning, Flower was awakened by the smell of fresh hot breakfast.

"Shawn," said Flower softly.

"Aye shorty, I laid out something for you. It's right there on the living room table."

Flower looked on the living room table and spotted a brand new white Nautica robe, a pair of Bugs Bunny stuffed slippers, one pair of Tommy Hilfiger boxer shorts for women, a brand new white T-shirt with the words "I Love New York" written in big letters and a brand new tooth brush. Flower just smiled.

"Here you go!" said Shawn handing Flower a plate of turkey bacon, scrambled eggs and grits. "I'll be right back with some orange juice for you."

"What's all the special treatment for, Chef-Boy-R-Dee?" said Flower stretching her back and arms.

"My Angel."

She yawned. "So I'm your Angel now?"

"You're not my Angel yet, but you will be," said Shawn smiling.

"And what makes you so sure about that?"

"Well for one, I'm the first guy who ever cooked breakfast for you besides your father. And number two, I put cheese in your eggs," said Shawn laughing.

"You didn't have to."

"It was my pleasure."

"Thank you Shawn."

"You're welcome."

"Tell me, why didn't you try anything with me last night? You had me all to yourself," said Flower fiddling with her food.

"Angel, you looked so relaxed. Plus, I didn't want to be disrespectful. The puppies were still awake, plus, I have plenty of time," he said smiling.

"Oh really?"

"Really."

"So do you cook for every girl that spends the night with you?"

"No, only the ones that spend the night with me because I like them and not just because I want to have sex with them."

"Why me Shawn? Out of all the girls in the club, why me?"

"I don't know Angel. I just have this feeling, that's all."

"Listen, I have to run, you can stay and get some rest if you'd like," he added.

"No, I'm okay. I have to take care of some things myself," said Flower. She took a few spoonfuls of the eggs, grabbed a strip of the bacon and stood up.

"Well can I see you again Angel?"

"Of course you can see me again Shawn," she said smiling.

"Is Angel your real name?"

"I don't think that matters right now Shawn. What matters is that I'm your Angel."

"No doubt, shorty. No doubt!"

Then they both got dressed and left the apartment.

CHAPTER FOURTEEN

District Attorney's Office, Bronx County ...

"Hey Murry, did you get a hold of Melinda Abrams yet?" asked Schnider.

"Not yet Schnider, I'm still getting an answering machine. I did get a hold of that Maria Rodriguez lady earlier," said Murry.

"Good, what did she say?"

"She said that we could come by anytime. She still opens the place up everyday from 6:30 a.m. to 11 p.m. We could go through there now if you'd like."

"Any pressure from Meyers?"

"Who, Javon's attorney?"

"Yeah."

"Nothing yet. I don't think she's too concerned with her client singing. She's an 18B, court appointed. She's actually a paid shithead, but must take on cases for free every now and then. I guess that gives her morals. And I hear that her main concern is to win cases."

"What about our guys in Ohio? Anything from them yet?"

"Sergeant O'Donnell is faxing me what he has as we speak. I figure, we go up to 211th Street and have a talk with Maria. By the time we finish with her, O'Donnell should have gotten us a full report."

"You ready?" asked Schnider.

"Let's go!" replied Murry.

"Weiner, take all messages pertaining to this Richardson guy and put them in the folder on my desk marked 'The Deli Shootings'," said Schnider.

"Okay Mr. Schnider. Anything else?" said Sheryl Weiner, Schnider's twenty-year-old African American paralegal and office secretary.

"No Ms. Weiner."

"Ms. Weiner?" said Murry.

"Yes Floyd."

"That coffee was delicious. Thank you!"

"You're welcome Floyd, and I told you that it's alright to call me Sheryl."

"Okay Ms. Weiner," said Floyd leaving the office.

"Floyd, ever since you fucked up and called Sheryl a weener, it's like she's had the hots for you," said Schnider as the two men buckled their seat belts in their brown Crown Victoria.

"I didn't call Sheryl a weener. I thought that was how she pronounced her name. And she doesn't like me. A crush maybe, but she doesn't like me. I'm too pale."

"I wonder what it'll take for an old white guy like myself to be able to attract women like you do."

"Remove your ring!" said Floyd as the two men head uptown to 211th Street.

211th Street and White Plains Road, The Salsa Deli …

Almost two years after the fatal shooting of her husband Eduardo

Rodriguez and her son Mario, Maria Rodriguez kept the family dream alive.

"Good afternoon Mrs. Rodriguez. I'm John Schnider, the assistant district attorney who's investigating the case on your husband and son. This is my assistant, Mr. Floyd Murry, my chief investigator," said Schnider introducing his partner.

Mrs. Rodriquez smiled. "Buenas tardes Señor? How are you?" said Mrs. Rodriguez.

"We're fine thank you. Mrs. Rodriguez, I went over the file on this case and I understand that it was a robbery that somehow went bad. Did you recover any dinero anywhere in or around the cash register?"

"My son Ramon came to the store after the shooting. I just started working here again for three months now."

"Can we get in touch with Ramon?"

"Yes, he's there!" said Mrs. Rodriguez pointing toward the rear of the store.

"Horhey, go and get tu hermano!" said Maria calling her son George in Spanish.

"Hermano, ven aca! Ahora! Come now!" said George calling his brother.

"Si Mama. ¿Qué es esto? ¿Qué paso hermano?" said Ramon asking his mother and brother what was going on.

"Ramon, this is the police. Talk with them," said Mrs. Rodriguez holding her son's hand.

"¿Qué paso señor? What's going on?" asked Ramon. He crossed his arms.

"Ramon, we just want to ask you a few questions." Looking at the men awkwardly, he nodded in agreement.

"Tu comprende Ingles?" asked Schnider.

"Si Señor, pero no mucho," said Ramon saying that he understood English, but not that much of it.

"The night that your father and your brother were killed, did you identify their bodies at the store or at the morgue? You know, the hospital place?"

"Oh, I know. No, I see mi hermano y mi papa on the ground behind la counter. They take their bodies away and then I clean up mi family store."

"The same night or did you clean later in la mañana?"

"I clean same night."

"Was dinero in register? Any money in machine?" asked Schnider, emphasizing his questions by moving his hands.

"Si, el dinero. The people no take the money."

"Si, all el dinero was there. They no touch," said Maria.

Looking at his notes, Schnider asked, "Mrs. Rodriguez, our records tell us that you don't know if your surveillance camera was working that evening. Was your camera working?"

"No, they took it."

"They took what? Who took what? Who's they?" asked Schnider.

"The people who kill my husband and mi son. They take la tape."

"So there was a tape?" asked Schnider with a quick nod of his head.

"Yes, si."

"Thank you Mrs. Rodriguez. Mucho's gracias. Thank you Ramon."

"Denada," said Ramon telling them they're welcome.

Schnider and Murry buckled up and headed for the highway.

"Floyd, are you thinking what I'm thinking?" asked Schnider.

"John, I believe I'm always thinking what you're thinking. Except when it's something dirty. But before we go choking up Mr. Richardson for that tape, let's see what our friends in Ohio have for us."

"Call Sheryl, see if she has anything for us," said Schnider.

Dialing their office, Sheryl picked up on the first ring.

"Hello, District Attorney's office, Sheryl Weiner speaking."

"Hey Sheryl, it's Floyd. Has anyone from Ohio called?"

"Yeah, a Sergeant Carl O'Donnell called and he faxed you some paperwork too."

"Did he say anything?"

"He just said that after you look over the paperwork, if there are any questions, feel free to give him a call."

"Okay. Thank you Sheryl."

"You're welcome Floyd."

Click!

"O'Donnell's faxed us something. We'll look over whatever he's sent us and then we'll determine how we'll have to go at Javon."

"No problem," said Schnider.

161st Street and Sheridan Avenue, The District Attorney's Office …

"It says here that Mr. Harold Dupont, also known as Bear, was in the Franklin County Jail in Columbus, Ohio serving thirty days for a suspended license. He was in custody from July 20, 1994 up until August 20, 1994 making it impossible for him to be present at that store on the night of August 6, 1994," said Murry.

"And what about Henry and Thompson, the other two that are alleged to have been there on that fateful night?" asked Schnider.

"Damion Henry had a motel checked out in his name that evening. Apparently he was having a party at the Knights Inn on Dublin and Granville Roads. The motel owner verified his picture from a photo array. He said he remembered Henry because the two of them got into an argument about how untidy the room had been left. Out of curiosity, O'Donnell also showed the motel owner Thompson's photo. He identified Thompson as one of the ones who kept making purchases from the vending machine that evening as well. Apparently Henry was having a welcome home party for Thompson. Jermaine Thompson was released from the Lucasville Penitentiary in Lucasville, Ohio on August 6, 1994 at 8 a.m., making it also very unlikely for him to be in New York the same day he was released from prison. Your boy Richardson lied to us Schnider," said Murry.

"I think we should pay Mr. Richardson another visit," said Schnider.

"Do you want to give Ms. Julia Meyers a call first?"

"I think we should find that tape and then hand Ms. Meyers the indictment against her client for those murders. In the meantime, find out if Javon had any stash houses anywhere."

"I'm on it!" said Murry.

"I know that tape is around here somewhere. It has to be!" said Schnider thinking to himself.

CHAPTER FIFTEEN

Tracy Towers ...

Flower quietly exited the elevator on the 27th floor. Remembering where the apartment was from the first trip, Flower walked over to it and tapped lightly on the door.

Tap! Tap! Tap!

After a few moments, Flower put her shoulder into it.

Boom! Boom! Boom!

Still, no answer.

Flower pulled out the Gucci key chain pouch and tried the first key. The key fit perfectly, but the lock wouldn't turn. Trying the next key, it also fit perfectly. This time, the lock turned. Flower opened the door and peeked into the dimly lit apartment.

"Hello, building management! Anybody home?" said Flower remaining at the door. Realizing that no one was home, Flower entered the apartment and locked the door behind her. Roaming from room to room, Flower searched the apartment high and low, checking every room from the living room and the kitchen, to the bedroom. In the living room, Flower searched under the pillows of the sofa and love seat. She searched the cabinets of the entertainment system, and the China cabinet that lined the hallway wall. "Nothing! Nothing worth taking," she thought. When she entered the master bedroom, Flower walked over to J.R.'s closet and opened it. She searched every article of clothing inside and out. Shirts, pants, shorts, she found nothing. She went through all of his shoes, still nothing! Getting frustrated, Flower plopped herself onto J.R.'s bed and stared into the ceiling. Admiring the ceiling's marble pattern, Flower followed the flow of streaks that all seemed to travel in the same direction. At one point, some of the streaks seemed to have gone in another direction, and then almost immediately, go back to the same flow of direction. Curious, Flower stood on top of the bed to get a closer look and realized that one of the ceiling tiles were set in another direction. Looking around for something that would extend high enough, Flower scanned the bedroom until she came across a black walking cane near the bed's headboard. She picked it up and poked at the ceiling where all the marble streaks were set in the same direction. None of them moved. She then poked at the single square foot tile that went in its own direction pattern wise. It moved. Flower almost pissed her pants as she let the cane fall to her feet. She looked around nervously for a moment as if someone could enter the house and catch her red handed. Realizing again that no one was in the apartment with her, Flower picked up the cane and shoved the tile to the side and noticed what appeared to be a small black strap. Flower hooked the cane to the strap and tugged on it. Down came a leather book bag that almost struck Flower in her face. She anxiously grabbed the bag and opened it hoping to hit the jackpot. Inside was a black semiautomatic handgun and a video tape. Flower placed the gun back into the bag, then shoved the bag to the floor. She got up and walked over to J.R.'s television and VCR set up and turned them both on. Flower slid the tape into the VCR. What first appeared to be a visual of security camera footage at a department store, seconds later was determined as being video surveillance of a small convenience store. Anxious as to why the video was hidden, Flower pressed the fast forward button hoping to find something until she noticed someone who looked familiar. She pressed play and then she pressed rewind until the person was exiting backward out of the store. She stopped the tape and pressed play again. Two seconds later, she saw the guy enter the store again. It's J.R., plain as day. However, instead of him being clad in his usual designer attire, J.R. was now draped in black jeans, a black sweatshirt and black leather gloves. He also wore a black wave cap over his head. As quickly as J.R. entered the store, a spark flashed and a man sitting on top of a ladder at the bottom of the screen was suddenly thrown to the ground. Flower pressed pause, then rewound the tape to where J.R. first walked in. Putting the tape on slow motion, Flower saw J.R. walk into the store and a flash from a black instrument that sat underneath J.R.'s left armpit is what caused the man on the ladder to fall off. It was a gunshot. J.R. entered the store and shot the man to his left with his right hand, concealing the weapon underneath his left armpit. Flower couldn't believe what she had just seen and almost threw up as she continued watching the tape. After hitting the man on the ladder, J.R. walked over to the counter and pointed the gun at two men standing behind the counter. It looked like he was motioning for the men to lay down on the floor. The man furthest to the right of the camera almost immediately complied, but the other man closest to the cash register waved his arms in front of the gun like he was pleading for his life. A flash appeared at the tip of the gun once again and the man who helplessly waved his arms back and forth pleading with J.R. for his life dropped to his knees and then backward as a single shot ripped debris from the rear of the man's head. Flower gasped as she witnessed the man who is accused of murdering her former lover, shoot a second man right before her eyes. The tape showed J.R. jump on top of the counter, then climb over it and stand directly over the other living store employee. Without hesitation, J.R. pumped three bullets into the head and face of the terrified victim. He then kicked both men in the face as if he were looking for a reaction from either one of them. Smiling, and clearly gratified by his heinous behavior, J.R. looked around the store's ceiling until he looked directly into the lens of the camera that recorded everything that just transpired. He smiled for the camera, admiring his work. Flower startled herself as J.R.'s creepy face left her with an eerie feeling. As Flower's nausea heightened, she leaned into the television to end the horrific tape when she noticed J.R. drop to the floor as if to hide from someone. Unable to control her tears that were to come, Flower sat there helplessly as she watched her father enter the delicatessen. She knew what was about to happen and began screaming at the television trying to throw the bedspread and sheets at it.

"No Daddy! No! Don't go in there! Get out Daddy! Get out! J.R., you bastard! Noooo!" she continued as the tears uncontrollably rolled down her cheeks. All her sobbing came to an abrupt halt when in walked Alize with the same exact outfit that J.R. was wearing. He too had a gun in his right hand. Raymond turned around and displayed a look of surprise as he came face to face with a 9 mm semiautomatic grimm reaper. He raised his hands in the air as Alize moved his mouth like he was speaking to the guy. Raymond slowly dropped his hands and kept them at his side. J.R. popped up and hopped over the counter and stood in front of Alize like he was taunting him and encouraging him to shoot. Both Alize and Raymond remained still like they were two statues. J.R. continued taunting Alize. Alize kept the gun pointed at Raymond's face, but never flinched at J.R.'s remarks. It was like he was in a trance. J.R. pulled his gun and walked over to Raymond and shot him in the head like it was nothing. When Raymond dropped, J.R. stood over his lifeless body and pumped five more bullets into his chest and abdomen. Alize lowered his gun, and stared at Raymond's body as the blood leaked from his head and onto the floor. In the background, J.R. ran around the store vanishing and reappearing into the camera's view until the video tape went fuzzy indicating that he had found where the tape was located. Flower couldn't hold it anymore, the thought of her father being killed was tremendously emotional. Witnessing it almost gave her a heart attack. Flower vomited all over the carpet and dresser in J.R.'s room. She screamed and hollered and cried! Flower even began swinging her arms wildly around the room knocking over a lamp and some picture frames, and breaking a mirror. She dropped to the floor and sobbed like a hungry baby.

After mentally being in another world for over an hour, Flower slowly regained her composure and walked into the bathroom to run some water in the bathtub. Her stomach wouldn't hold so she pulled her pants down, sat on the toilet and began moving her bowels in the form of diarrhea. Flower then washed herself up and pulled her hair into a ponytail. She went back into the bedroom, pulled her Fendi sunglasses out of her purse, placed them on her face and grabbed her jacket. Flower also put the tape into her purse. She picked up the gun and tucked it into the sleeve of her jacket, and without looking back, Flower left J.R.'s apartment pondering on her next move. Flower caught a taxicab on Jerome Avenue and called Rosalyn from her cell phone.

Ring! Ring!

"Hello, Ms. America speaking!" said Rosalyn excitedly into the receiver.

"Rosalyn," said Flower, still emotional from watching the tape.

"Flow, are you okay? You never call me Rosalyn. Ever!"

"No, I'm not okay Rosalyn," said Flower with firmness in her tone.

"Talk to me girl! What's the matter?" said Rosalyn sympathetically. Flower began crying again.

"Flower! Flower! Talk to me! Talk to me!" said Rosalyn, becoming more and more nervous as they talked.

"Ros, I saw my father," said Flower in a monotone voice over her tears.

"You saw your father?"

"Um hmm."

"Flower, Raymond is dead! Don't be going crazy on me girl! I told you that club shit was going to get to you!"

"Rosalyn, I seen my father on a video tape being shot." Flower glanced at the taxicab's rearview mirror and caught the taxi driver staring at her. She kept her eyes glued to his until he focused his attention back on the road.

"A tape? What? Flower, you're not speaking with a clear mind right about now. Have you been drinking?"

"Rosalyn, I haven't been drinking and my mind is about 80% clear. I'm talking to you at this moment in a sane state of mind and to prove it, I'll describe what's going on right now. I'm riding inside of a cab that I caught on Jerome Avenue. My name is Flower Abrams and my mother's name is Melinda."

"Alright, alright, already! So what the hell is going on?"

"Ros, I was just over J.R.'s house." Flower wiped the tears from her face.

"I thought J.R. was in jail?"

"He is."

"So how the hell were you over at his house?"

"I snuck in! I had his keys, remember?"

"You snuck into that man's house? What the hell is wrong with you girl? You done lost your damn mind! You done went from a stripper to a burglar!"

Flower sniffled. "No I didn't, I was just snooping around looking for shit."

"Snooping around? For what?"

"Money Rosalyn! Jewelry! Anything!" she said raising her voice.

"Did you find anything?"

"I found that tape that I've been trying to tell you about. It showed when my father got shot at that store."

"What, how! I mean, did you see it Flower? Did you see your father actually get shot?"

"Yes Rosalyn. I seen them kill my father."

"Oh my God! Are you, are you okay?"

"I will be," she said sniffling again.

"Did you see who did it? I mean, maybe the police can arrest somebody now."

"The person who did it is already in jail."

"Who? They caught him already?" said Rosalyn sounding surprised.

"Rosalyn, J.R. and Alize went to kill my father. Alize wouldn't pull the trigger so J.R. shot him. I don't think Alize had the guts to kill my dad. He knew I loved him despite all the … Never mind."

"Despite all the what Flower? Tell me! Despite what?" Rosalyn was pushing for information.

"Ros, I'm downstairs now. Come outside and I'll tell you. I'll tell you everything."

Flower shut off her cellular phone.

"How much Mr.?" she asked.

"Fifteen dawless," said the African cab driver.

Flower gave the man a five and a ten dollar bill. Two minutes later, Rosalyn was outside in her slippers. She saw Flower hiding behind her sunglasses and realized the seriousness of it all.

"Are you okay girl?" asked Rosalyn giving Flower a hug and patting her on the back.

"Hold up Ros," said Flower pulling away from her friend. "Let's walk because I know all of these nosy mothafuckas are probably all in my mouth from their windows," she added.

The two young ladies walked south on Park Avenue toward 168th Street.

With her arms crossed and her handbag draped over her shoulder, Flower began to confess. "Ros, Raymond used to rape me."

"What!" Rosalyn stopped in her tracks and stared at her best friend.

"All the time. Since I was nine years old," said Flower continuing to talk.

"Oh my God Flow. That's sick!"

"I know, trust me, I've been reminded over and over again. Do you remember my 9th birthday party that I had at the Skate Key?"

"Yeah."

"That was when it all began. I was so scared Ros and I couldn't do anything about it. He was too big and too strong. He even tried to drown my ass in the tub. He said he would kill me had I said anything to anybody. He made sure his sick ass washed me up good afterwards too. That nigga didn't want anything up in me that could be traced back to his ass. I probably would've went and told somebody but what kept me quiet was when he said that he'd hurt my mom."

"He said that he would hurt Mrs. Melinda?"

"Um hmm. He said that he would hurt me too, but I couldn't be hurt any worse. My father violated me Ros. So one day, like right before he got killed, I met Alize. We hit it off and I told him what my father was doing to me."

"He raped you from the time you were nine years old up until he died?" Rosalyn was shocked. She couldn't believe what happened to her close friend.

"Um hmm."

"He only died last year Flow."

"I know."

"What! Why you ain't say anything to me?" said Rosalyn, stopping in her tracks again.

"I had to keep it my secret. It went on for too long and I thought people wouldn't believe me. So I just let it continue, praying that one day he'd get tired of me and leave me alone."

"I feel so bad Flow." They continued walking.

"Don't Ros. It's over now. It's finally over."

"So what did Alize say about it?"

"He basically said that my dad would pay for his actions one day. I never thought it would end like this though."

"How are you feeling right now Flow?"

"I don't feel anything Ros. I've done been through it all. I've been through everything. That's why I act the way I do. I don't know what's right or what's foul. Or what love is," said Flower beginning to cry again. "I just know how to have sex. When a man violates you like that, who you think loves you more than he loves himself, it has an effect on you that is really hard to imagine.

"Wow, that is so crazy."

"And if it never happened to you, that's all you can do. Imagine!"

"So what are you going to do with the tape? You do know that you may eventually have to tell your mom about all of this."

"I know. And she might blame me for everything too."

"No she won't Flow. She'll understand. I promise!"

"I know that before I hand this tape in to the proper authorities, I will sit down with my mom and tell her everything."

"Are you going to tell Shawn about any of this? Because for some strange reason, I think he really likes you."

"I don't know. I really don't know him like that yet. We never slept together or anything."

"You didn't? I thought you said the man cooked you eggs and bacon and shit," said Rosalyn, causing Flower to chuckle.

Flower shrugged her shoulders. "He did, but we didn't do anything. We just chilled."

"Do you think he might be the one?"

"The one for what?"

"The one to slow your ass down!"

"I think I've had enough running around. You know, enough is enough. I can't take anymore drama. I'll go crazy. This tape shook my ass up and made me think about my life. It's time for me to take a chill pill."

"You ain't gonna dance no more or nothing?" asked Rosalyn.

"Nope, I'm going to go and see the girls one last night, then I'm going to see what's up with this Shawn character. I'm going to see if he's the one."

"I heard that! Well, we've done circled the block two times. Let's go and get us something to eat. You hungry right?" asked Rosalyn.

"I don't think I can eat anything right now Ros. But I'll have a Snapple iced tea."

"That's my Flow. Let's go!"

CHAPTER SIXTEEN

At home, Flower tried to mentally and emotionally maintain her composure and keep her head level. She called her mother at work and paged Mrs. Berkowitz. She told them both that it was urgent and that she needed to speak with them at home as soon as possible. It was the early part of the evening and Mrs. Melinda would be home soon anyway. Always willing to lend a hand, Mrs. Berkowitz accepted the invitation and was getting ready at home. After a long shower, Flower sat on the bed, looked in the mirror and asked herself, "How do I tell them what happened? Will they believe me or blame me?" she thought.

Flower hadn't been to church in years and thought she had forgotten how to pray. Her mom always told her, "Whenever you feel like talking to God, just get on your knees, close your eyes, and block everything else out." The time had finally come and Flower knew she needed the strength from the Creator to build up the courage to tell her mom and Mrs. Berkowitz her traumatic story. Flower slid her feet out from her slippers, dropped down to her knees and leaned into her bed. She closed her eyes and began praying to God, hoping that he would listen. "God," she began, "Creator, I really don't know where to begin. I don't know if I've been a bad person or if I've been a good person. I know that I have done some stupid things in my life, but I never did anything with intentions on hurting someone else. I really loved my dad, and I don't know if he was a sick person or simply a mean person. He never gave me a spanking before I turned nine years old, and he never yelled at me before either. I hope all the times that I asked you to stop him from hurting me, that you didn't answer me with his death. I only wanted him to get help if he was sick. I don't understand why I loved him when he did so many terrible things to me. Maybe it's just a child's love for their parent. I do ask that you give me the strength to confront my mother with the news and that you allow her to accept this information without it ruining what she and I have left. God, I ask that you continue providing me with the strength and guidance I need to keep me on the straight path of positivity. God, I also ask that you protect me from the pain and the agony of the guy below. I hope that you will forgive me for the sins that I may commit in my future. Before I finish, if you're listening to me, which I know you are, I ask that you watch over my dad's soul. I ask that you watch over my mom, Mrs. Berkowitz, Rosalyn and her family, the girls at the V.I.P. Club, and if Shawn isn't the guy for me, help me overcome that as well. Amen!" Flower opened her eyes and felt better than she had in a long time. She pulled her hair back into a ponytail, put on a pair of sweatpants, a T-shirt, and waited for her mom and Sarah to arrive.

"Hello," shouted Mrs. Melinda entering her apartment.

"Hi Mom," said Flower running over to her giving her a firm hug and a kiss.

"What was that all about?" asked Mrs. Melinda.

"Nothing. I just haven't shown you any love in a long time, or told you how much I care about you."

"I'm listening," said Mrs. Melinda smiling.

"Mommy, I love you so much. I miss kicking it with you and

everything."

"Flower, are you pregnant?" asked Mrs. Melinda backing away from Flower with a frown sprawled across her face.

"No Mom! No!" said Flower pulling her mom closer to her again.

Tap! Tap! Tap!

"It's me, Sarah," said Mrs. Berkowitz outside of their apartment door.

Melinda opened the door and greeted Mrs. Berkowitz with a hug and a kiss.

"Hey Sarah, how are you?" asked Mrs. Melinda.

"I'm fine Melinda. And yourself?" said Mrs. Berkowitz entering the apartment.

"Wonderful, just wondering what Flower is so anxious to talk about this evening."

"Well Mom, I called you to come straight home and I invited Mrs. Berkowitz over because I want to talk to the both of you about the dreams that I have been having."

"What's the matter, are they getting worse Flower?" asked Mrs. Melinda, obviously concerned.

"No Mom, in fact, I hardly even have them anymore. Mrs. Berkowitz has been such a blessing and I would certainly like to thank her for everything and commend her on tolerating me," said Flower, looking at Sarah.

"First of all Mom, I need you to promise me that you'll hear me out and be open minded about the things that I'm about to tell and show to you."

"Show me what Flower?" asked Mrs. Melinda firmly.

"Mom!"

"Melinda, let her finish. It's time for us to be the ears. All we're to do is listen, and be patient. We're her friends right now," said Mrs. Berkowitz nodding her head.

"Okay honey. I'm sorry. Continue sweetie. And I promise to keep quiet until you want me to speak," said Mrs. Melinda.

"Mom, Sarah, when I was nine years old, I was raped."

"What! My God!" said Mrs. Melinda.

"Melinda!" said Sarah, looking to her to calm down.

"I'm sorry, oh my," said Mrs. Melinda, visibly shaken by the news.

"Mom, please!"

"Go ahead darling. I'll handle your mom," said Sarah, clutching Melinda's hand.

"Daddy raped me Mom. He raped me up until the time that he died," said Flower beginning to cry. "I never said anything because at that tender age and that happening, I was confused. I didn't know left from right. I knew something was wrong, but because it was Daddy, I thought there must be an exception. I would also blame myself a lot, until I got to know Mrs. Berkowitz here. Mrs. Berkowitz helped me understand more about rape and the victims of that heinous crime and the effects it can have on us. I realize now that we live in a crazy world and that things happen Mom. There are sick people out there who will take advantage of a situation, manipulate others and take what they want, especially from a woman. I realize now that I can only help myself through self-analysis, prayer and the encouragement from my loved ones. Amazingly, Mom, I've developed and blossomed into a bright, strong young lady. Also, though I'm not proud of it, I have been sexually active with other guys, but today, my life is changing."

Mrs. Berkowitz sat beside Melinda rubbing her back, keeping her calm as her tears continued to pour from her eyes.

"Mommy, one of the guys that I called myself associating with had this at his house," said Flower showing her mom the tape. "And no Mom, I am not on this tape," said Flower, as her mom relaxed. "However, what is on this tape is very disturbing. A couple of weeks before he died, Daddy attempted to molest me again, but I managed to avoid it. Doing so, I met a guy from the neighborhood named Alize. Alize was really a nice guy. I told him what Daddy was doing to me and he wanted me to go to the police."

"Why didn't you come to me?" asked Mrs. Melinda.

"I was afraid Mom. Let me finish! Anyway, I told Alize that my dad didn't deserve to go to prison. Me being naïve I guess. But Alize took it personal. He wanted to kill Daddy. But he couldn't do it, so his friend did it for him. Mommy, I feel so bad because, had I told someone, maybe Daddy would've stopped and would still be alive today."

"Flower, God is the creator of life and he takes us when he needs to. You had nothing to do with your father being killed. He brought that on himself," said Mrs. Melinda.

"So what's on that tape?" asked Sarah.

"This tape shows when my dad got shot in that store."

"No!" said Mrs. Melinda shockingly.

"And I don't know what to do with it."

"Does it show who shot your father?" asked Sarah.

"Yes. This guy named J.R. He's in jail now but not for shooting my dad. He shot the other guy, Alize. That's what he's in jail for."

"Melinda, don't look at that tape. It's not good for any of us," said Mrs. Berkowitz.

"I seen it," said Flower.

"Are, are you okay honey?" asked Sarah.

"Yeah, I'm okay now. It was scary and it made me throw up and everything, but it also brought me to this point so I'm okay now."

"Wow, Flower, you're an amazing young lady. I thank God that you're okay," said Mrs. Berkowitz.

"Yup! So what do we do with this tape?" asked Flower.

"Melinda, do you still have the telephone number to the detectives that covered Raymond's case," asked Sarah.

"I believe so. Ironically, the investigating detectives have recently been trying to contact me. If I'm correct, the messages should still be on my voice mail." Melinda picked up her phone and punched in the code to check her messages.

"You have two messages!" said the computer.

Beep! Melinda pressed the button to begin checking the messages.

"Melinda, it's me Sarah."

Beep!

"Your message has been deleted," said the recording.

Beep!

"Hello, this is Mr. Floyd Murry of the Bronx district attorney's office. At your convenience, please contact us at 555-1873. It's regarding your late husband."

Click!

"5-5-5-1-8-7-3."

Ring! Ring! Ring!

"Hello, District Attorney's Office, Ms. Weiner speaking," said Schnider's secretary.

"Good evening ma'am, my name is Melinda Abrams. I'm returning a call from a Mr. Floyd Murry."

"Hold on please."

Click!

"Floyd, you have a call on line one!" said Ms. Weiner.

"I told you we were through for the evening," shouted Mr. Murry.

"Floyd, pick up the phone! It's Melinda Abrams."

"John, it's the Abrams lady," said Murry excitedly.

"Hello, Mrs. Abrams?" said Floyd on speaker phone.

"Yes, is this Mr. Floyd Murry?"

"Yes ma'am. I've been trying to reach you for some time now. There've been some strange developments regarding your late husband's murder."

"I see. Well, I've come across some strange developments myself."

"You have? Would you mind sharing that with us Mrs. Abrams?" asked Murry, looking over at Schnider.

"Why don't I come over to your office and meet with your people."

"If it's no problem for you Mrs. Abrams."

"It's no problem. It'll be my pleasure."

"Fine."

"I'll be there in twenty minutes."

"Do you know where our office is?"

"I've been there before. When Raymond first got killed."

"We'll see you then."

"Bye."

"Bye, bye Mrs. Abrams."

Click!

"Come on Flower. Come with us too Sarah. They want us to come down to their office and talk with them. Are you up for it Flower?"

"Yes Mommy."

"You sure you'll be okay? They may want to go over the tape in your presence," said Mrs. Melinda.

"I'll be fine. I can handle it," said Flower.

"Well put your shoes on and let's go! Bring that tape Sarah!" said

Mrs. Melinda.

161st Street, Sheridan Avenue …

Melinda pushed the buzzer for Suite #2.

Buzzz!

"Yes," said Ms. Weiner.

"Mrs. Abrams."

"Sure, come on up."

Click! The door unlocked.

Walking up the stairs, Mrs. Melinda, Flower and Mrs. Berkowitz were greeted by Ms. Weiner.

"Right this way," said Ms. Weiner, leading the women to a large office.

"Thank you," said Sarah, as Ms. Weiner returned to her desk.

"Have a seat ladies," said Schnider. "This is my partner, Mr. Floyd Murry," he added, as Murry proceeded to shake the women's hands. "And this is Homicide Detectives Robert Chin and Michael Philips. They are the lead detectives on the case involving your late husband. Now before we proceed, you said over the phone that you may have something for us."

"I do," said Mrs. Melinda reaching for the tape from Mrs. Berkowitz. "This here is the tape from the store that my husband was killed at," she added, passing Mr. Schnider the tape.

"Where'd you get this from? We've been trying to locate this tape since the beginning of this investigation," said Detective Chin, a tan complexioned guy who stood 6', 190 lbs., born to an African-American mother and a Chinese father.

"Go on Flower, tell them," said Ms. Melinda.

"I was seeing the guy who's on that tape. He's in jail now, but not for shooting my dad. Anyway, I went to his house and I found this tape. He had it hidden in a bag in his ceiling. I watched the tape and brought it straight to my mom and asked what should I do. She suggested that we call you guys. So here we are."

"Sheryl, would you bring the T.V./VCR set up in here please?" asked Schnider. "What made you look in this guy's ceiling? Were you trying to hide something up there yourself?" he asked.

"No, I thought I was his girlfriend so I was searching for clues to prove my theory that he was cheating," said Flower lying.

"Oh, I see. Flower, is that your real name?" asked Schnider.

"Yes sir."

"That's a beautiful and unique name," he said.

"Here you go sir!" said Ms. Weiner, plugging the set up.

The assistant district attorney along with his chief investigator and the two detectives all sat in awe as the tape played, showing the gruesome murders of Raymond and the three Latino store employees. Melinda couldn't hold back her tears so Sarah gave her the support she needed by holding Melinda's hands tight and rocking side to side with her, whispering in her ear, "It's okay Melinda. Everything is alright."

After shutting off the monitor, Schnider began to speak. "I think we have ourselves an indictment fellas."

"Looks like it to me," said Murry.

"We agree," said Chin, speaking for both him and his partner.

"First thing in the morning, I'll go over to the court house and have a talk with Judge James Chapman. Then I'll call Ms. Julia Meyers with the news about her client. Once we put the paperwork together, I'll notify you Chin, and give you the okay to tell the Rodriguez family. Flower, if this idiot decides to go to trial, we may need you to testify. Is that okay with you?" said

Schnider looking at Flower and her mom.

"Yes," said Mrs. Melinda as Flower nodded in agreement.

"Mr. Schnider, will you guys have to establish a motive for these killings now that you know that the motive wasn't robbery?" asked Mrs. Melinda looking over at Flower.

"This tape is all that we need," said Schnider.

"Thank God," whispered Sarah.

"Thank you so much Flower. That was very brave of you to come forward like you did. And thank you for coming by Mrs. Abrams."

"Thank you," said Mrs. Melinda.

"Oh, Mrs. Abrams, we'll keep you posted on the case. And if you need trial dates or anything, Ms. Weiner will call you with all of the details. I'm pretty sure though that we won't need any testimony from Flower. This should be enough to get us a conviction and put Mr. Richardson behind bars for the rest of his natural life," added Schnider.

"Bye, bye," said Sarah.

"Take care. And thanks again," said Murry.

"Hey John, you want some coffee?" asked Murry.

"Sure, why not," said Schnider.

"Come on Sheryl, join us for some coffee," said Murry.

"I'll be ready in a jiffy Floyd," said Ms. Weiner.

They all hopped into Murry's car and headed for the diner.

CHAPTER SEVENTEEN

The V.I.P. Club!

Celebrity Night ...

"Aye Cinnamon, guess who's in the house?" asked Cherry.

"Who? Rappers or athletes?" asked Cinnamon, answering her friend with a question.

"Ain't that Big Man and them from Brooklyn," asked Cherry pointing at a group of rappers in one of the booths.

"Yeah, that's him. Him and his little crew. What they call themselves, The Mini Cartel or something, right?"

"I don't know, but I like his CD that's out. It's called I'm Ready to Live. He got some party shit on there. I'm about to go over there and make me some rap money," said Cherry.

"I'm coming too," said Cinnamon following behind Cherry.

"Angel, where've you been at girl? I've been worried about you. Ain't none of us seen you in a few days. Is everything okay?" asked Mt. Everchest.

"Yeah, everything's cool. I think this is going to be my last night here Eve," said Flower.

"How come Angel? I was just beginning to like you and get close to you. Damn! Every time I find somebody that I can kick it with and not worry about whether or not the bitch is jealous of me, she up and leaves. Is it that guy you've been seeing?"

"Not really Eve. I've just been taking into consideration all of the things that you and I have been talking about lately as far as getting my shit together is concerned."

"I heard that."

"Eve, do you even know how old I am?"

"You're probably around nineteen Angel, but you act like you're thirty," said Mt. Everchest laughing.

"Eve, I'm only fifteen."

"Fifteen?" said Mt. Everchest shockingly.

"Well, I'll be sixteen next month, but I'm too young for this shit. I have to chill, you know what I'm saying?"

"Girl, had I known you were only fifteen, I would've barred your little young ass from the club my goddamn self. So what, you going back to school or something? Time to get your shit together?"

"Yeah. I've been through so much that it's pathetic. I need to slow my young ass down while I still have a chance."

"Are you going to keep in touch with your girls?" said Mt. Everchest holding her arms out looking for a hug.

"Of course Eve," said Flower responding. "Y'all are my girls. Even though Cherry and Cinnamon be acting like they don't care about a bitch, I still got love for them."

"Angel, you want to know why they be acting like that around you? They're mad because they started out young just like you. Cherry was fourteen when she started. Cinnamon was sixteen. They started out together.

That's why they stick with one another like they do. Now they're twenty-six and twenty-eight with two bad ass kids a piece and no baby daddies. So it hurts them when they see a girl like you come into this lifestyle when you got your whole life ahead of you."

"Why didn't they leave?"

"They weren't as strong as you are Angel. You should've seen you when you first got here. You were so firm. You held your ground. Never once did you fold under pressure either. Both of them had bad experiences when they first came into the game. They started out doing little bachelor and house parties and they slipped up when they started fucking guys at the parties. Word got out that they were two sisters who were willing to fuck for a fee. Then some guys got an abandoned house and made it seem like it was their own shit. They called up Ebony and Ivory, which were their names back then, and when they got there, all hell broke loose. One of the guys let them in, then two guys grabbed Cherry and Cinnamon from behind and dragged them into a back room. They were each bound and gagged to a bed that lay side by side one another. And for two whole days, guys from all over went up inside every hole in those girls. Cherry and Cin were so delusional from the pain that half the time they thought they were dreaming or that it had been days that they were there. They were allowed to use the bathroom and were also given water and Chinese food, but it was back to the casting couch after that. Both of their rectums were torn and they had every venereal disease you could name. They were a mess Ange. So it hurts them when they see people like you that are so pure and clean. They want to be you. They want that innocence back."

"Damn! Did the guys ever get caught who did that to them?"

"Some of them niggas probably frequent this place to this day. They wouldn't know. They never seen any of the guys' faces."

"Well, they shouldn't judge a book by its cover because if they knew half of the shit that I've been through, they'd change their minds about wanting to be in my shoes."

"If you were one that has been to hell and back, you sure don't look or act like it. Most of the time, you're smiling."

"Eve, I smile to keep from crying. It's all a façade. But I'm ready to move on so I'm going to make this money tonight and keep it moving."

"Just don't forget your girl Ange. I ain't going anywhere for a while, unless King Tut comes to get me," said Mt. Everchest smiling. "Go on girl, do your thing!" she added with a tear dropping from one eye.

Flower walked around entertaining customers and taking their money like a loan shark on a mission. She entered a booth that had the fat white guy from the previous night who was still sweating and still in his green suit.

"What's up Big Boy?" said Flower.

"What's up bitch! You want me? Huh? You want this green machine?" he said nervously.

"I'll be your bitch alright. How much money do you have on you?"

"This is all I have," said the guy waving a small wad of one dollar bills.

"Oh yeah, well let me see then!" said Flower slamming the guy up against the wall of the booth and searching his pockets. Flower pulled out a roll of $50s wrapped in a rubber band and said, "Are you being a naughty boy? Are you hiding shit from me?"

"Yes ma'am. I've been a naughty boy. I'm sorry!" said the guy dropping to the floor. He voluntarily pulled his own shirt up to his chest and pulled his pants to his ankles and got into a doggie style position.

"Spank me! Spank me bitch! Please!" he pleaded.

Flower looked around but couldn't find anything.

"Give me your goddamn belt you fat mothafucka!" she demanded.

The guy complied and Flower whupped his ass cheeks like he done stole something. Flower would cock her arm way behind her back and give it all she had over and over again until his behind looked like a large tomato. After dropping the belt and tucking her money, Flower strolled around and stopped when she came upon the same white lady who she caught licking on Mt. Everchest and who also claimed to not eat dark meat.

"Hey! Hey white lady!" shouted Flower.

Turning around smiling, the lady responded by saying, "Young lady, I thought I told you before that I wasn't interested. Aside from me eating swine, the other white meat, I only feast on Mt. Ever …"

Flower cut her off by grabbing the poor old lady by the jaw and shoving her onto the booth's sofa.

"Oh my gosh! Young lady, are you out of your mind?"

"Mary Poppins, you need to shut your damn mouth before I do something that'll make it have to be wired shut! Aretha! Aretha!" shouted Flower.

"Yes!" said Aretha walking over to the booth.

"Aretha, this bitch right here says she loves her some dark meat. She said that it's the next best thing since swine. Why don't you tell her what your name is," said Flower balling a fist up at the terrified lady.

"Well sugar, my name is Aretha Spanking!" said Aretha, a 350 pound black woman with a triple "F" bra size. "And I loves me some pigs feet, Hog Mog, chitterlings and white women," she added.

"Why don't you let her taste your stuffing then ma!" said Flower.

Aretha took off her silk robe and fully nude, bent over on the table in the booth. She grabbed her butt cheeks with both hands and pulled them apart as far as she could.

"Look here little white lady, I don't have all day. So bring your cracker ass over here and do what you do best!" said Aretha.

"Bbbbbbut," said the lady stuttering.

"But nothing bitch! Now if you don't stick your face where the sun has never shined, I'm going to sit my big ass on the same spot you sit your reading glasses. Now come on!" said Aretha making the lady jump and run over to her rear.

The lady began licking like a kitten with his first bowl of milk.

"Bitch, if you don't get your tongue out of my pussy right this second, I'm going to turn around and knock your little ass out," said Aretha.

"I thought this is what you wanted Ms. Aretha," said the white lady, even more terrified than before.

"Lick my asshole bitch! Only my stinking ass husband is allowed to feast on this salmon. Come on now, get back in there!"

Screwing her face up, the white lady complied. She licked her rear until her jaws were numb.

"After you get done with all that crack, my cheeks could use a washing too!" she added.

That's when the lady fainted.

Flower's Bed

CHAPTER EIGHTEEN

Flower laughed and walked away.

"Hey girl, what are you doing?" asked Mt. Everchest.

"I'm looking for Cherry. Have you seen her?" asked Flower.

"They in booth 20."

"Her and Cin?"

"Um hmm."

Flower made her way to booth 20 and called Cherry's name. "Cherry! Cherry! Cinnamon! Are y'all two in there?"

The music was so loud and the girls were so caught up in their activities that no one heard or saw Flower enter the booth.

"Uh, uh, uh, uh, uh, uh, uh, uh!" Flower couldn't tell who was making the most noise. Both women were getting double penetrated by four guys. Flower could see Cherry clutching a few hundred dollar bills so she knew they were taking care of business.

"Flow, go out, I'll talk to you later!" said Cherry, a little embarrassed and still getting worked over.

Flower walked out of the booth caressing her temples. "This shit is crazy. I can't wait to get out of here," she thought.

On her way to the restroom, Flower spotted Freaky peeking from one of the booths.

"Hey cutie," said Flower walking over to Freaky.

"Hey shorty. I thought I scared you off," said Freaky.

"As long as I'm getting paid, don't shit scare me."

"So are you ready for another episode with Big Freaky Fo Sheezy?"

"I don't think you can handle this," said Flower.

"You don't think Freaky can handle you? Big Freaky is the Freakiest of all Freaks. I can handle anything."

"So let's go in the booth and see what you're made of."

They walked into the booth and Flower began to dance.

"Take your shit off Freaky!"

Freaky took off all of his clothes except his shoes and his socks. He grabs his Vaseline packet and begins applying the substance to his penis.

"Hey Freaky, you want me to do that for you? You never know, I might accidentally sit on it while I'm at it."

"Yeah, yeah, come on! Do your thing girl!"

"Let me see your tie."

"My tie, for what?"

"Because, I'm a freak too. I like it when you use your imagination. So why don't you take that tie and wrap it around your head."

"You want me to blindfold myself?"

"Um hmm."

Freaky tied his tie around his head and Flower tightened it, making sure that he couldn't see.

"Now lay on your back," she said softly.

Freaky lay on his back as his member slowly began to rise for the occasion.

"I'll be right back," said Flower.

"Where are you going?"

"I need a drink. Now lay your ass back down before I change my mind."

Flower ran out of the booth and looked high and low until she spotted her target.

"Aretha! Aretha! Shouted Flower.

"Hey Angel," said Aretha strolling toward her. "Good looking out on that lick, literally," she said laughing. "That little white bitch did a number on me. Now all I need is a big fat dick and I'm straight."

"Guess what girl?"

"What?"

"I got this guy who said he wants a whole lotta woman, if you know what I mean! And he's at least 10 ½ inches easy. There's only one catch ma."

"What's that?"

"He wants you to jerk him off a little bit and then he likes for you to ease on top of him like you're sneaking and taking the dick. He has this thing where he wants to feel like he's being raped. He'll fake it by trying to fight you off, but he really wants it. So go and give it to him good Aretha."

"How much is he paying?"

"I don't know. He gave me this," said Flower pulling out the wad of 50 dollar bills that she took off of the green machine, the fat white guy in the green suit.

"Take me to him now!" said Aretha.

Flower walked Aretha over to the booth where Freaky was blindfolded, lying on his back and gently stroking himself.

"I'm back!" said Flower.

"Took you long enough!" said Freaky.

"I told you I had to get big momma warmed up right?"

"Yeah, you said that."

"So shut your freaky ass up and enjoy!"

Wiping his hand across his mouth as to demonstrate that it is zippered shut, Freaky then placed his arms at his sides and grinned.

Aretha walked over to Freaky and palmed the head of his shaft. She then began stroking him gently as she eased herself over top of him without releasing his member. Assuming that her vagina was positioned right over the head of his penis Aretha used her huge leg muscles to slowly lower herself onto Freaky's shaft. She teased him at first by only allowing the head of his member inside of her. After a few short strokes, Aretha couldn't take it anymore. She slammed all 350 pounds on top of Freaky causing him to gasp. He yanked the tie from his face and screamed at the sight of the 350 pound woman. Looking over at Flower, he screamed, "Heeellpp! Heeellpp!"

Flower just walked out. But before she disappeared past the curtain, she looked over at Aretha and said, "Make sure he cums good big momma. Otherwise, he might want his money back."

"Oh big momma is going to make him cum alright. Right up in big momma," said Aretha humping away.

As the evening ended, all the ladies got word that it was Flower's last evening at the club. They all gathered together in the dressing room and shared a few words of encouragement for her departure.

Cinnamon lit a cigarette and blew out a cloud of smoke. Then she gave Flower her blessing. "Angel, good luck to you sugar. You have your whole life ahead of you. Go out there and make somebody happy. You're a good girl and you deserve a good life," said Cinnamon.

"Aaww! Thank you," said Flower walking over to Cinnamon and sitting on her lap. "You deserve a good life too Cin. Better than what your life is like now. All you have to do is put your mind to something. Focus on it and set your goals. Once you reach your first goal, nobody's going to be able to stop you. And your kids need you too," she added.

"Girl come here!" said Cherry. She was sitting alone on a love seat. Flower walked over and sat down next to her. Cherry hugged her and kissed her on her forehead. "My grandmamma used to kiss me on my forehead all the time. She told me when someone kisses you on your forehead, it means that you're special. You're really something Angel. We're going to miss you fo sho. And don't worry about me and Cin, we're big girls. We can handle ourselves. I know you've seen us doing some crazy shit and I hope and pray that it doesn't fall back on our kids." Crying, she continued, "I know I ain't shit, but all I got is my pussy, my kids and my best friend Cinnamon. I ain't never had love, because to me, it don't exist. But I do have a heart because it hurts me to see you leave. It's all for the better though, and I don't want to see your ass back here talking about it's hard out there. You get yourself together girl and you find yourself a good man and be the best wife that you can be to him. And have some babies too because I know you'll be one heck of a mother," said Cherry sniffling.

"Thank you Cherry. I appreciate the compliments. And I also, over the course of knowing you, realize why they call you Cherry. It's because you are so sweet mamma. All of you are!" said Flower looking around at all of the girls. "But Cherry, you're unique. I got faith in you girl. I know you're going to snap out of this bullshit one day. Just don't look back when you do. Okay!" said Flower kissing Cherry on her forehead. "You're special too. That's why your grandma used to kiss you there," she added.

"Come on over here youngster!" said Mt. Everchest with her arms stretched out. "You should've been the one that everyone called Eve. Shiiit, you're the only angel around here," she said laughing. "I don't really have too much to say. Definitely, stay your ass in school! Get you a job where you're comfortable and make you some money. After you get yourself enough money, go down south somewhere, where the cost of living is cheap. Buy you a nice little house, a fat ass ride and just sit back and kick it. Take your ass to church, where we all should be at every Sunday," said Mt. Everchest pointing around the room, "and just chill girl. Keep your head up, don't let shit get you down and never, ever give up on something that you really want. If you can see it, you can achieve it," concluded Mt. Everchest, hugging Flower.

Flower responded. "Eve, I have never met anyone quite like yourself. I mean you're white, but you're cool," said Flower causing laughter amongst the group. "Plus you're big as shit," she said, making the girls laugh harder. "But I love you girl. I love all of y'all in here. And I know that we all can make it. Trust me, I'm making it. Or at least I'm going to make it. I've been through my own drama too. Right Eve? I know what happened with you and Cinnamon," said Flower looking over at Cherry. "It happened to me too. And for five whole years. From when I was nine years old up until a little after my fourteenth birthday, my father raped me on a regular basis." The girls were stunned. They couldn't believe it. "But I put my faith in the Creator and He gave me the strength to get past it all. I'm good now. And spiritually, mentally and emotionally stronger than ever. So take it from me, we can all overcome adversity. Just think, it could be worse. We could all be dead. So let us come together and pray, and ask the good Lord to guide us," said Flower.

The girls huddled up and Flower lead them in prayer. "God, please guide all of us as we travel in this crazy world. Help me and my friends get our lives back together. When the road gets rough, show us the smooth route. If the load gets too heavy, help us carry it, and never place a burden on us that we cannot bear. Amen!"

Everyone gave one another hugs and kisses and the ladies all left the club. Flower caught one of the taxicabs that frequent the area and rode home alone. She entered her apartment and prepared herself for a shower. After taking her shower, Flower placed all of her club outfits into the trashcan and climbed into bed. She cut the light off, turned on her radio and fell asleep. For the first time in a long time, Flower slept like a baby. And not once did a bad dream enter her mind.

CHAPTER NINETEEN

MDC, BROOKLYN ...

Inside the housing unit, inmates busied themselves with a variety of prison activities. J.R. and three others were engaged in an intense game of spades.

"Kneecaps, you know it's over for you and your partner right?" said Ashcan, a 5'7", 165 pound black guy with burns over 60% of his face.

"Yeah whatever! Me and Bullet are about to run a ten on you guys as soon as your partner Jay Easy here deals us this bubble," said Kneecaps, a skinny Puerto Rican dude with a long rap sheet for stealing and stripping cars.

"Let's get it popping then! Jay, how many books do you have?" asked Ashcan.

"It's on them to bid first. I dealt remember?" said J.R.

"Oh yeah. Y'all asses are mine! I should run a ten on you guys by myself," said Ashcan, fixing his hand.

"Bullet, how many books do you have?" asked Kneecaps.

"I have a funny hand right here. I need to bid off of you," said Bullet, examining his hand.

"What's score?" asked Kneecaps, causing all of the players to look at the score.

"It's tied up, twenty-nine/twenty-nine. So you and your man have to go a seven or better in order to beat us, and according to my hand, you guys are going to need a miracle. As a matter of fact, we'll let you two cop out right now and just give us twenty-five pushups," said Bullet.

"I got two books. Two and a shot, maybe," said Kneecaps.

"You don't have three? Tell me that you have three books and we're going to spin 'em!" said Bullet referring to a bid of ten books, which is the highest bid you can make when playing spades.

"Shiiiit, the way you're talking, I might as well have three. So fuck it, count me for three!"

"Spin 'em! Spin them!" said Bullet asking for the ten book bid.

"How many books do you have, Can?" asked J.R., with a concerned look on his face.

"I don't have shit! Nothing! Nada!" said Ashcan.

"Nothing? I thought you were going to run a bubble on them all by yourself," said J.R.

"Nigga, I was bluffing! How many do you have?" asked Ashcan.

"Fuck it, give us the board. I'm a gambling man. Y'all two are going to have to make me a believer," said J.R. referring to a bid of four books, the lowest one can bid in a game of spades.

"We don't even have to play this," said Bullet, showing the rest of the players his hand.

"What, what's going on? What are you doing?" asked J.R.

"Look son, he don't have any clubs, I got the whole family of those. He only has one diamond and one heart. And his partner got tops in those two suits. This nigga got eleven trumps. Who the fuck has the other trump? I know I have the three of spade," said Ashcan referring to the money suit of the game.

"Yeah! Yeah, nigga!" said Bullet. "Lock mine out!" he continued referring to the fifty pushups that Ashcan and J.R. have to do for losing the game.

The guys got down and began doing the pushups when the correction officer, Ms. Grant, appeared over the P.A. system.

"Richardson! Javon Richardson! Report to the officer's station!"

J.R. stopped before he reached fifty and his opponents demanded that he continue until he was done.

"That wasn't fifty!" said Bullet.

"Yeah, get the rest of that money!" said Kneecaps.

Continuing to walk away, J.R. yells out, "Get it like Tyson got his! In blood nigga!"

Reaching the officer's station, J.R. asked the officer why was she calling him.

"Yo C.O.! What's up?"

"Yo C.O.! Mister, I think you need to get it straight! It's Ms. Grant, not 'Yo C.O.'! Now what do you want?"

"You just called me on the jumpoff."

"The jumpoff. Listen, I'm not with all the slang stuff. Some of us in here are educated you know. What's your name?"

"Richardson."

"Get ready. You have an attorney visit."

"I am ready. I just need a pass."

"Give me your I.D. then."

J.R. passed his identification card to Ms. Grant and she copied his name and identification numbers onto the pass.

"Here you go!" said Ms. Grant passing J.R. his pass. She buzzed him out and he headed for the 'Receiving and Departure' area of the facility where all attorney visits, interrogations, etc. are held.

"Floyd, do you think he'll be stupid enough to take this to trial?" asked Schnider.

"He seems stupid enough. But if he has any sense at all, he'll accept this plea for four consecutive sentences of life without the possibility of parole. Either way, he's fucked. Except if he goes to trial, then we kill him. But if he cops, then he kills himself," said Murry.

"What if he tries to give up something else?"

"He doesn't have anything else to give. Otherwise, he would've given it to us before he gave us the deli shootings."

Tap! Tap! Tap!

"Your inmate is here," said R & D officer Dirken.

"Let him in please," said Murry.

J.R. entered the room.

"Is my attorney here?" asked J.R.

"I thought she would've notified you already," said Schnider. Schnider had his secretary inform Ms. Julia Meyers about the new indictment against her client, at approximately the same time that he and Floyd would be serving her client his new indictment. They also brought along homicide detectives Robert Chin and Michael Philips to re-arrest J.R. on the charges.

"No, no one notified me about anything. Is this about what we talked about?"

"Well yeah, in fact it is," said Schnider. "However, there have been some changes due to new developments," he added. "Why don't you guys tell him the good news," said Schnider to Chin and Philips.

Chin opened a black pad and said, "Javon Richardson, you are under arrest for the quadruple murder of Eduardo Rodriguez, Mario Rodriguez,

Miguel Nunez and Raymond Abrams who were shot and killed on August 6, 1994 at the Salsa Delicatessen on 211th Street and White Plains Road. You have the right to remain silent Mr. Richardson. Anything you say or do can and will be used against you in a court of law."

"I know all of this bullshit already," said J.R. frustrated and confused.

"You have the right to an attorney. If you cannot afford one, the state will provide one for you," said Officer Chin closing his pad.

"Schnider, can you please explain to me what's going on?" asked J.R.

"Yeah, we have evidence on a tape that points the finger in your direction. It proves you shot those people," said Schnider.

"Y'all don't have shit on me! And this case would've still been unsolved had I not given you the information I had. You can't flip it on me. Ness and BG did it and my lawyer will prove it."

"Suit yourself Richardson. You shouldn't have been dumb enough to give us that information in the first place. We're cops; we don't give a damn about you or any other criminals out there. This is merely a job for us. So when you deal with us, always remember that we will do our best to fuck you while getting what we want," said Schnider. "Let's get out of here! Fingerprint him at court tomorrow during his arraignment," he added.

Assistant district attorney John Schnider, his partner Floyd Murry and detectives Chin and Philips exited the Federal Detention Center and headed back to their offices to prepare the necessary paperwork to try the case. J.R. was escorted back to his unit where he acted like nothing ever happened.

"Jay, where'd you go, to a visit or something?" asked Ashcan.

"Nah, I was at the clinic. Fucking nurse has the nerve to tell me that I'm not sick."

"Are you?"

"Nah, hell nah! I was just bullshitting to get out of the unit for a while. A nigga needs a stress walk every now and then. Na mean!"

"Yeah, I got you. You want to run another game of spades against these bums?"

"Nah, I'm tired Ash. Hold it down by yourself, ya heard!"

"Yeah, I'll just get me another partner until you're ready."

"Ah-ight."

"One!" said Ashcan, telling J.R. Peace Out.

J.R. walked over to his cell and placed a cover over his window letting his cell buddy know that he's either using the toilet or doing something more personal like masturbating. He sat on his bunk and began unlacing his shoes as he thought about the authorities finding the tape. He pulled the laces from his shoes and placed his shoes underneath his bed. He connected both strings together at their ends and formed one end of the strings into a noose. He then climbed on top of the toilet bowl and tied the other end of the string to the air vent that hovers over the toilet. Tugging on it to make sure it'll hold, J.R. then placed the string around his neck and closed his eyes.

"I'd rather die than be trapped in a living hell!" said J.R. before hanging himself.

J.R.'s cell buddy discovered his lifeless body during the afternoon count and the paramedics were called in to try and revive him. They were two hours too late. J.R. died of asphyxiation by hanging himself in his cell.

"I guess that closes the Deli Shootings case," said Schnider after receiving the news about J.R.'s suicide.

"Yeah, I guess so. And I was right. Mr. Richardson wasn't stupid. That kid was sick!" said Murry.

"Let's notify Maria Rodriguez and Melinda Abrams about the news

Floyd," said Schnider.

"Okay, you take care of that while I go and get us some coffee and doughnuts."

"Don't forget to call Samuels and Ross at the bureau. They'll need to know what happened to Richardson as well. Perhaps those Ohio kids will now take a plea for killing that Barrow kid," said Schnider leaving the office.

"Yeah, but that's out of our hands. Our case is done and over with."

CHAPTER TWENTY

450th East 169th Street

One Week Later …

"Flower, how come you're not sweating any cars that are driving by?" asked Rosalyn.

"Girl, you know I gave that shit up," said Flower.

"So what's up? How'd your mom feel about all the drama. Them finding out who killed your dad and then the killer taking his own life?"

"I think she's handling things okay. Mrs. Berkowitz has been at the house a few times this week offering her support. So we're getting over all the B.S."

"What's up with Shawn? Have you spoken with him lately?"

"I just got off of the phone with him. He's on his way over here now. We're supposed to be going out. When we sit down somewhere, I'm going to ask him if he's ready to settle down because I'm tired of running around myself. I want to finish school, get me a good job and if I have to, I'll do it all single. I don't think I need any distractions anyway."

Beep! Beep!

Shawn blew his horn as he pulled up in front of Flower's building.

"Ros, I'll call you tonight. I'm going to hang out with the mystery man for a little while," said Flower.

"Call me!" said Ros.

"I will!" replied Flower as she climbed into Shawn's Lexus.

"What's this, a 300 or a 400?" asked Flower, referring to the model of Shawn's car.

"It's a 300. The SCs don't come in 400 yet. What do you know about 300s and 400s anyway?" asked Shawn.

"I love cars. I know a lot of the new ones that are out. American cars don't do anything for me. Unless it's a truck like a Tahoe or a Yukon. Other than that, I'm strictly European. Know what I mean?" said Flower smiling.

"You're amazing, you know that?"

"I know. Now where are you supposed to be taking me?"

"Actually, I have the whole day planned out for us. First we'll go to the Bronx Zoo. The rest of the day will be a surprise."

"The zoo?"

"Yeah, the zoo. It'll be fun. It's romantic when you're with someone that you really like and care about."

"So you really like me?"

"After this week is over, you tell me," said Shawn leaning over planting a kiss on Flower's cheek.

They headed for the Bronx Zoo and Flower had the most fun she'd had in a long time. They visited the monkey pen and made funny faces at the different kinds of monkeys. They then visited the elephant arena, but ran up out of there when an elephant passed gas leaving an outrageous odor. The two of them also fed a few ducks and goats with peanuts you buy from a candy machine. Flower laughed when she learned how goats will eat anything, even the paper bag that the peanuts come in. The couple watched a set of bears mating and they also watched some trainers put on a show with some specially trained dolphins. After leaving the zoo, Shawn and Flower took a romantic ride through Central Park on a horse and carriage ride. The horses would walk and move their bowels causing Flower to cringe in her seat at the thought of horse manure right in her face. She frowned at the idea that workers were paid to shovel the stuff up until she learned they were earning twenty dollars per pound of manure. After the horse ride, Shawn took Flower to a movie theater in Soho which showed pornography films on its big screen. The movies would only last thirty minutes per segment, but by the time the movies would end, Shawn, Flower and every other couple in the theater would be making out for the umpteenth time. They left the movie theater and realized that they hadn't eaten all day.

"Flow, let's go uptown and grab a bite to eat," said Shawn, walking over to the driver's side of his car.

"Where do you want to go and eat?" she asked.

"I loves me some soul food."

"Me too," she said entering the vehicle.

"Let's go up to The Shark Bar then. They got these delicious Soul Rolls. I'm telling you, you're going to love them," said Shawn rubbing his hands together like he were starving and the food was just placed in front of him.

"Where's the Shark Bar?" she asked.

"The Shark Bar is on 74th Street and Amsterdam Avenue."

"What's the atmosphere like in there? Am I dressed appropriately?" she said, looking down at her outfit.

Flower had on a pair of Donna Karan New York sneakers, a pair of Donna Karan jeans and a Donna Karan shirt.

"You're alright. It ain't no black tie affair type of thing. There's always celebrities up in the spot though. You'll easily see a rapper or an R&B

singer up in there on any given day. And the owner doesn't discriminate. A nigga out the hood has money that spend just like a nigga with a recording contract. It's small as shit in there though."

"So what's their Soul Roll thing that you're talking about is the bomb?"

Shawn started his car and eased into the flow of traffic. "It's like a big patty and it's stuffed with rice, black eyed peas, collared greens and your choice of beef, chicken or turkey. It's banging ma, I'm telling you."

For the next several days, Shawn gave Flower the Key to the City. Among other things, the two of them slept in an exquisite suite at the Trump Plaza Hotel in Manhattan every night they were together. They would begin the next several days with room service, usually a hot breakfast and separate bubble baths to make them feel important. That next day, Shawn took Flower on a shopping spree at Macy's and Bloomingdale's allowing her to run up a bill of over $10,000. She purchased some of the finer things in designer clothing such as Dolce & Gabanna, Fendi, Gucci and Prada. That afternoon, they went up to the Jacob Javitz Convention Center for their annual car show. They took pictures next to and inside all of the latest prototypes. Flower sat inside of every Mercedes Benz and BMW and took several pictures. She also took a few pictures standing near the new Yukons and Tahoes. Her best picture of the afternoon was when she posed like she was Marilyn Monroe in front of a classic styled Rolls Royce and Bentley. Before calling it an evening, they stopped off at the One Fish Two Fish restaurant located on 91st Street and Madison Avenue. There they had smothered Whiting with macaroni and cheese. The next day, the day after that, and the day after that were all just as exciting. And each evening always ended with a gourmet dinner at places like the Motown Café which is located on 57th Street and 5th Avenue. There they had some delicious fried chicken with rice an peas and they watched

Motown artist impersonators perform classical Motown hits. Wilson's, which is located on 158th Street and Amsterdam Avenue was another spot for them to enjoy some soul food. There they ordered chicken and waffles and drank pink lemonades. They also visited the V & T Restaurant on 110th Street and Cathedral Avenue for some of their fabulous veal parmesan. The last day they spent together on their New York City tour, Shawn and Flower rode the Manhattan tour bus, they took the Circle Line Ferry to and from Staten Island, they visited the Statue of Liberty, the Museum of Natural History and the Aircraft Carrier Museum at the South Street Seaport. Then they took a $175 per every fifteen minute ride on a helicopter that toured the entire city. It flew them up and down the Hudson River and landed on a helipad that sat adjacent the famous Windows on the World Restaurant on 12th Avenue.

"Wow Shawn, this week has been very, very interesting," said Flower as they walked into the glamorous restaurant. "I never flew in a plane before, let alone a helicopter. And why am I being treated like royalty?" she added as the elevator reached the top floor of the building.

"Your stop sir, ma'am," said the elevator man.

"Thank you," said Shawn, handing the man a tip.

"Thank you," said Flower following suit.

"Sir, do you have a reservation?" asked a male employee at the restaurant's front door.

"Yes, my name is Shawn Moore, and I have my guest with me."

Finding his name, the man said, "Right this way Mr. Moore."

Showing Shawn and Flower to their seats, "Would you like something to drink sir?" asked a casually dressed waiter.

"Yes, I'd like a club soda please."

"Ma'am?" asked the waiter.

"Make that two of them. Thank you," said Flower pulling herself close to the table.

"I'll be back with your appetizers and ready to take your orders shortly."

"So, you were about to tell me what the deal was with you doing all of these extraordinary things with me," said Flower smiling.

"Flow, I'm a firm believer in persistence. I strongly believe that if you want something bad enough, you go right out and get it. And from the first day I laid eyes on you in that club, I wanted you. And I prayed that I'd have you," said Shawn.

"You prayed to have me. Why didn't you just ask me?" she frowned.

"I didn't ask you because look, I met you in a strip club. The first impressions weren't the best you know. You were a dancer, I was a customer. I figured you'd think I'm some kind of pervert. Plus, I didn't really know what to think when I saw you except that you were one of the most beautiful women I ever seen in my life. So I asked the Creator to help me out with this one."

"So do you think He granted you what you requested?"

"I don't know yet."

"What do you mean you don't know yet?"

"Sir, ma'am, here are your drinks and appetizers. Are you ready to order yet?" asked the waiter.

"Did you see what you'd like to eat?" asked Shawn.

"Why don't you continue being a gentleman and order for me," said Flower.

Shawn looked at the waiter and said, "Okay, Mister, may we have two orders of your Super Snow Crab Legs with two side orders of fried shrimp."

"Will you be having desert with that sir?"

"Yes, give us two apple pie ala modes. That should be all. Thank you," said Shawn to the waiter winking at him signifying not to mess anything up and he'll receive a nice tip.

"Sooo, what do you mean when you say you don't know if the Creator granted you what you requested? I thought spending a week together and sitting here with me right now would automatically answer your question for you."

"Flower, did we have sex yet?" asked Shawn.

"No, and that's another thing. Not once did you try anything with me. Even when I had my bra off, all you did was cuddle up against me. And I know that you're very much into women because you're very much into me, but I was beginning to wonder …"

"What, that I was gay?" asked Shawn cutting her off and laughing. "I can assure you that ain't nothing gay over this way. And the two reasons why I didn't touch you was for one, the question that I asked the Creator and two being the feelings that I have for you."

"Well you not touching me didn't seem too right. So what are your feelings toward me since we're on this topic?"

"Flower, I asked the Creator could he one day make you my wife."

Flower gasped. "I don't know what to say Shawn."

"You don't have to say anything yet. And as for my feelings toward you, the reason I didn't touch you in a sexual manner was because I was trying to see if I could fall in love with you for who you are without the influence of sex. And you know what Flower?"

"What Shawn?"

"It worked. I'm in love with you regardless of everything that has happened to you in your past. I didn't tell you this, but I found out where you live. I drove through 169th Street one day and I saw this girl. I inquired about you and I guess she thought that I was your boyfriend because she and I sat out there for about an hour talking about you. Coincidentally, the girl turned out to be your best friend, Rosalyn, and because of my sincerity, she opened up and told me about everything that was going on with you recently. That's why I wasn't around for a minute. I was trying to give you your space."

"Excuse me, Mr. Moore, your food sir," said the waiter, placing all of their dishes on the table. "Anything else Mr. Moore?" he asked.

"No thank you," he said to the waiter letting him walk away. "So anyway, I found out about Alize, that kid J.R. and Mrs. Berkowitz. I even know about your father Flower. And I will tell you right now that no matter what the outcome of our relationship turns out to be, I will always be your friend and in your corner. I promise you that!"

Flower had never been spoken to like that by any other man. The beautiful thought of being somebody's wife gave Flower the chills and filled her eyes with tears of joy.

"Well since you know so much about me now and you say that you love me, how do you feel about my age?"

"I know you'll be eighteen in two years and right now you're very mature. So age isn't a factor."

"Okay."

"Ladies and gentlemen, Windows on the World will start rotating in sixty seconds. Please enjoy your evening," said the manager over the intercom.

"What's going to happen in sixty seconds?" asked Flower.

"You'll see. Watch!"

About one minute later, the whole top floor of the restaurant began to slowly rotate, giving all its customers a great view of the greatest city in the world. The evening progressed with Shawn and Flower dancing a little bit and then retreating to their hotel suite. Flower entered the room first and blushed at the idea of their room being flooded with scattered pink and yellow rose petals. A bottle of Crystal champagne lay on either sides of the king size bed on the two end tables in buckets of ice. Luther Vandross played low on the room's hidden speakers, and Shawn had the lights dimmed giving the room a more romantic feeling. Flower turned to him and placed her lips on his and shoved her tongue into his warm mouth. Shawn returned the favor as he tiptoed over to the bed with her still in his arms. He removed his clothes all while never releasing his grip from Flower. Shawn had Flower lie on her back and told her to spread herself out like an angle. He pulled a bottle of warm honey from the microwave and pulled its cap off with his mouth. "Close your eyes my sweet little Angel." Then he proceeded to pour the honey all over Flower's body with a damp towel at his side. Shawn licked most of it off and wiped off any spots that he couldn't get to. After that, he had Flower sit up and eat two chocolate covered cherries from his fingers, and to his surprise, Flower sucked on every one of his fingers after doing so. Shawn gently shoved Flower on her back and grabbed her by her ankles. He elevated her legs and sucked every toe thoroughly before making his way up to her love tunnel. He got to her vagina, kissed it and patted it giving her the tease of her life. He then backed up and placed her legs on his shoulders entering her vagina slowly. Shawn and Flower made love well into the morning in every position they could think of. They went from the missionary position on the bed to them standing in the middle of the room with Flower bending over grabbing her ankles as Shawn slid in and out of her from behind. At one point, they made love on a chair with Shawn cocking Flower's legs as far east and west as they could go. He then stood Flower up and pressed her front side up against the wall while he penetrated her once again from the back. They ended their evening, early morning love session in the hot tub where the bubbles weren't the only thing that Flower swallowed.

That week together marked a new beginning for the two love birds. They became inseparable and kept each other happy all the time. When Flower would become sick, Shawn would make her feel better. And whenever Shawn needed advice on something, Flower was his consultant. The nightmares were over and life seemed to be one big happy dream. Whoever thought something would go wrong.

CHAPTER TWENTY-ONE

Two Years Later … 1997

Flower and Shawn had moved to suburban Reading, Pennsylvania, and the two were now doing extremely well with their lives. There were rarely any problems between the two of them and they were engaged to be married on Flower's nineteenth birthday. With the money that Shawn made from his street dealings, combined with the loan they secured from the bank, the couple purchased two eight-family brownstone buildings calling one 'His' and the other one 'Hers.' Flower served as the buildings' landlady while Shawn took the position as the superintendent. The rent money they accumulated monthly paid the mortgage on their Pennsylvania manor, an 8,800 square foot home located in the heart of the town's greatest recreation area. Their home luxuries included hand-hewn rustic oak flooring, granite countertops, wormy butternut cabinets, and extensive use of slate and travertine. Two master suites with Jacuzzi tubs, four additional bedrooms, two-and-a-half additional baths, a river rock fireplace and a theater room complimented their exterior and beautiful landscape.

At this point in their lives, with things working out so smoothly, the couple figured it was a great time to visit relatives back at their old Bronx neighborhoods.

Sitting at the foot of their bed, Flower expressed how she was feeling. "Shawn, I think we should drive up to see my mom. I mean, ever since I've gotten my life together, all I've been able to do is share the happiness of my success with my mom over the telephone and through photographs. Rosalyn even stopped coming to visit. She's probably spending all of her time getting to know her new boyfriend," said Flower.

Shawn was leaning over tying his shoes. "Oh yeah, I forgot she broke up with your arch enemy. What was his name, Raheem or something, right?" asked Shawn.

"Yeah, I never did like his fat ass. He always thought he was a hard rock and a thug," said Flower crossing her arms.

"So what's up with this new guy, does he sound like he's a good dude?" he asked leaning back up.

"He seems like it, but he's West Indian. And West Indians are very possessive." Flower looked into her fiancé's eyes with a look of disgust.

"What is he, a Trini or a Jamaican?"

"He might be a Trini because he still has his accent. Rosalyn told me that most Jamaicans lose their accents after they're here in the United States for a long while."

"How long has he been here now?"

"According to her, all of his life."

"He's probably a Trinidadian then," said Flower and Shawn together.

"So are you ready to go up to New York today?" asked Shawn.

"Yeah, let me grab my keys and my purse," said Flower walking over to her closet.

"That means it's fronting time. I gots to hit up the Big Apple with my shines on. A nigga can't be a baller without the jewels hanging in New York.

And Flower, you can wear my big chain with the big circle medallion on it," shouted Shawn.

"That thing is too big. It's all heavy and stuff."

"Well just bring it anyway. I'll put it on when I get to your mother's building."

"What time is it?" asked Flower.

Looking at his Oyster Perpetual Rolex with the day and date, it said four o'clock.

"It's like four o'clock Boo!"

"So we should get there around seven or seven-thirty depending on how fast you're going right?"

"Yeah."

"Alright, I'll be ready in one second. Let me grab my jacket just in case it gets chilly up there tonight."

"Don't forget my chain!"

"I'm not going to forget your chain Shawn!"

Shawn decided that they should drive his brand new Toyota Supra to insure a quicker ride. They jumped on Interstate 80 and headed east for New York.

New York City, 7:45 p.m.

Shawn and Flower pulled up in front of Flower's old building at almost eight o'clock that evening.

"Damn Flow, it ain't no parking spaces in front of your mom's building," said Shawn.

"Well double park right here and put your hazard lights on. I'll call my mom from the car and tell her to come outside. I'll call Rosalyn's cellular phone too and tell her to meet us over here."

Flower began dialing her mother's number as she and Shawn sat double parked right outside of the building.

"Ayo son!" said an unidentified male. "That Supra got Pennsylvania tags on it. Homie is probably copping some of that shit!" the unidentified voice continued.

"Do you want to get them," asked another unidentified male.

"Hell yeah!"

"Let's get them then!"

The two unidentified males walked over to Shawn's Supra as Flower was about to leave a message on her mother's voice mail.

Beeeeep!

"Hello Mom, it's me."

Before Flower could finish her message, both men were on either side of the vehicle with their guns pointed into the car.

Click! Click!

"Listen here Player, let me hold that!" shouted one of the males pointing his gun back and forth at the car and at Shawn's face. The other male had his gun pointed at Flower's face.

"You won't be needing these keys for a while!" said the guy pulling the keys from the ignition. "And while you're at it, let me get that watch, that bracelet, that chain, those rings and that bulge in your pocket! Yeah that too Homie!" said the male pulling off all of Shawn's jewelry from him. "Nigga, get that bitch out of the car while I strip this faggot. I want to see his bama ass hit that corner and act like he's Jesse Owens!"

For a minute, Flower was beginning to recollect because the words she just heard sounded familiar. However, she was too afraid to think quick enough. Shawn's cell phone began to vibrate on his hip as he exited the car. When he went to press the power button to end the vibrating, the last thing he heard was, "This nigga got a gun!"

Then the shots rang out …

As Flower slowly opened her eyes, her vision appeared fuzzy and cloudy at first. Then she noticed all of the machines that were connected to cords and wires. She followed one of the wires from one of the machines and it met in the bend in her right arm. One of the other cords went from another machine and connected to a small cup that covered her nose and mouth. Her mind began to wander when she noticed all the flowers that were in her room.

"Where am I?" she thought. "Am I in a hospital? What am I doing in a hospital? What happened to me? Where is everyone? Where's my family? Where's my mom? Where's Shawn? Am I okay?" she continued.

Flower began to panic. Then she saw the door open and heard a familiar voice.

"Sarah, ask Rosalyn can she grab me a spoon. I forgot to grab one. I need it to stir my coffee," said Mrs. Melinda.

"Mom," said Flower whispering.

"Baby, you woke up," said Mrs. Melinda whispering back. She put down her coffee and coffee cake and sat in the chair next to Flower's bed. "Easy Flower. Take it easy. Everything is alright now."

"Mommy, what happened? Where am I?" she said trying to move.

"You're in the hospital darling."

"What happened to me?" asked Flower as Mrs. Berkowitz and Rosalyn were entering the room.

"Is she up ma?" asked Rosalyn.

Turning around, Mrs. Melinda told Rosalyn that she was awake.

"Thank God!" said Mrs. Berkowitz praying out loud.

"Rosalyn, Mrs. Berkowitz, what's going on? Where's Shawn? Mommy, where's Shawn?" said Flower nervously looking around.

"Flower you were shot. Somebody tried to kill you. Thank God that you didn't die!" said Mrs. Melinda.

"What! When? By who? And Where's Shawn?"

"Calm down sweetheart. Some crazy people robbed you and Shawn in front of my building three days ago. They shot both of you."

"Well where's Shawn?" asked Flower with tears welling up in her eyes.

"Ma, let me talk with her," said Rosalyn. "Flower, Shawn is upstairs in the Intensive Care Unit. Unfortunately, he was hit more times than you were."

"Where was I hit?"

"One shot hit you in the chest, but you were wearing some big medallion that blocked the bullet that would've killed you. The doctors said that you were lucky to be alive. They said a couple of more inches to the left, and the bullet would've pierced your heart," said Roslyn.

"You were also hit in your shoulder honey. Apparently, these guys were trying to kill y'all, but were obviously bad shooters. The doctors had to remove the bullet from your back because it traveled when you were hit. That's why you probably feel pain in your lower back area. They operated on you for fourteen hours honey. And me, Sarah and Rosalyn were right outside that door. We certainly weren't leaving your side," said Mrs. Melinda.

"Is Shawn going to die?" asked Flower. "Please tell me."

"Flower, Shawn is in a coma!" said Rosalyn.

"What!" said Flower crying now.

"They shot him twice in the head, once in the stomach and in both of his arms. Flower, Shawn was supposed to die where he laid at. He's still here with you. That means a lot Flower," said Rosalyn.

"Who did it?" asked Flower.

"No one knows. The police have been around, but you guys were out cold."

"What are people in the streets saying?"

"Nobody saw anything."

"Well who found us?"

"It happened right in front of the building. Somebody nosy that lives on the front side of the building probably saw something. But right now, nobody's cooperating. I was coming from the store when I seen all of the commotion," said Mrs. Melinda. "I didn't know it was you all because I didn't know what kind of car you guys were driving. But I seen Rosalyn over there jumping up and down screaming. That's when I got scared. She looked over at me and ran right into my arms. You should've seen her Flower. This girl loves you to death. She was hollering and screaming talking about, 'They shot my sister, they shot my sister!' So at first I'm like, 'Calm down! You don't have any sisters.' But when she said your name, I broke fool. I blacked out too. They told me that I had to be restrained. I guess I was brought here with you because I don't remember coming here on my own."

"What hospital am I in?"

"They brought you here to Bronx Lebanon."

"Isn't this place a dump? Patients were dying left and right in here years ago."

"It was, but it's gotten better over the years. They remodeled the outside of it and everything. It looks nice now. And apparently they got themselves a new staff with some better doctors because they saved you and Shawn."

Hearing Shawn's name, Flower became sad again. Shawn became

the world that she orbited.

Tap! Tap! Tap!

"Excuse me, Mrs. Abrams," said Detective Philips, walking in with his partner Chin.

"Oh, hello detective. She's up now," said Mrs. Melinda standing up to greet the detectives. "Honey, Detective Michael Philips here and his partner Robert Chin are handling this case. They were glad that I gave them a call, otherwise you would've gotten some lazy bum asking questions for nothing."

"Hello," said Flower.

"I called them because I was satisfied with the way they handled Raymond's case, plus, we were familiar with them. I hope you don't mind dear," said Mrs. Melinda.

"No Mommy, it's okay."

"Flower, do you mind if we ask you a few questions?" asked Detective Philips as Sarah and Rosalyn exited the room.

"I don't mind. Ask me whatever."

"A few nights ago, you guys drove from your home in Pennsylvania. Did you guys come alone?"

"Yes."

"Did anyone know that you were coming to New York?"

"Only my mom. I told my friend Rosalyn that I was coming down, but I never gave anyone an exact date or time because Shawn and I didn't exactly know when we were coming. It had to be something on a humble."

"It appeared to be a robbery. Did your boyfriend have on a lot of jewelry?"

"Yes. He had on his Rolex watch, his Rolex bracelet, a necklace with a pendant and a diamond ring on both of his pinky fingers. He also had a diamond stud in his ear."

"We recovered his earring and his cellular phone. And we also recovered the necklace and damaged pendant that you were wearing. It's down at forensics being examined. As soon as we're done with it, you'll get it back. Apparently the other stuff was stolen. Was all of his jewelry platinum?"

"Yes, everything. And everything was encrusted with diamonds."

"The reason we ask is because we have people in pawn shops all over the city who work with us in cases like this. When you find the strength, let us know exactly what this merchandise looks like."

"Well we have photos and receipts at home. I'll get you that stuff when I'm released. Mom, how much longer will I be here?"

"The doctors said you could be released as early as tomorrow. Your shoulder and your back is all stitched up, but they decided to keep you on the I.V. for one more day to prevent infection," said Mrs. Melinda.

"Well Mrs. Abrams, Flower, nice talking to you guys. Flower, I hope you get well soon and we'll be in touch," said Detective Philips. He and his partner walked out of the hospital ward scribbling notes into their note pads. They headed back to their station house to put together the clues they collected.

"Mom, am I able to use the restroom or do I have to go through these tubes?" asked Flower.

"You haven't been to the bathroom since you've been here. You've been asleep the entire time. But if you have to go, the restroom is right outside this door to your left and it's the fourth door on your right."

"What about the mask? Can I take it off?"

"You can remove the mask, but the I.V. has to stay in your arm until morning. It's connected to this thing right here," said Mrs. Melinda showing Flower the I.V. stand. "You see, it has wheels on it," she added.

"Help me up," said Flower.

"Don't worry, we got you," said Sarah, entering the room and lending Mrs. Melinda a hand with getting Flower out of the bed.

"I got it now. Let me walk by myself."

Flower exited the room and walked toward the restroom. She continued past the restroom and walked onto a waiting elevator. A doctor was on his way to another floor and Flower figured it was a perfect time to question him.

"Excuse me sir, I seem to be a little lost. My room is on the same floor as the intensive care unit is, but I wandered off and got lost. Could you tell me where I have to go?"

"Sure, it's on the 7th floor ma'am. And make sure you don't lose your I.V. You can lose some of your strength if it's out of your arm long enough," said the doctor.

"I'll be careful. Thank you."

Flower got to the seventh floor and found her way to the intensive care unit. She read the names on every room until she came across the name that was most important to her – Shawn Moore. He was in the coma section of the ward with two other patients who had succumbed to that helpless state of deep unconsciousness. The other patients were either white or Hispanic so it wasn't hard to identify which body was Shawn's. Shawn's head had swelled up to an enormous size because the bullets that struck his cranium, pierced an organ in his skull causing blood and other fluids to clog up arteries in his brain. His eyes appeared to be sealed shut with blood and though his body seemed lifeless, his torso moved up and down with the help of an apparatus indicating that his body was still alive. Flower felt her legs beginning to shake as though they were about to give out when the elevator door opened and out came Mrs. Melinda, Sarah and Rosalyn running to her aid.

"Flower, we had a feeling this is where you had gone," said Rosalyn.

"Girl, you can't be scaring us like that," said Mrs. Melinda.

"Sweetheart, it's not healthy right now for you to be seeing Shawn in his current condition. You don't need the memories of seeing him like that if he didn't pull through," said Sarah. That's when everybody looked over at Shawn's helpless body and reality began to set in.

"He is going to pull through. He has to," said Flower crying in her mother's arms. "He just has to!"

CHAPTER TWENTY-TWO

Flower was released from the hospital the following afternoon. Her flirting with a male nurse allowed her opportunity to visit Shawn before she left. Flower was told that she couldn't touch Shawn but before she left, she kissed him on the lips and told him that she loved him. Upon entering the coma unit, Flower asked her mother, Mrs. Berkowitz and Rosalyn to wait outside. She walked over to her fiancé who was hooked up to four monitors, gently grabbed his hand and began talking to him.

"Shawn, I love you more than anything in this world. We've been through so much together and I don't know how I'm going to manage if you leave me alone in this crazy world. You are my right hand and I am your left. When you and I first met, I thought I wasn't good enough for you. I was this loose, promiscuous little tramp doing anything for nothing. You showed me the way Shawn. You taught me how to respect myself and be a woman. You were that shoulder for me to lean on and I won't ever give up on you. I will stay by your side until we're both laid to rest. They tried to shut us down when they robbed us, but we were superheroes that wouldn't die. So listen here Superman, Superwoman pulled through, I know you will too. I need you to be here with me Shawn. I really, really need you here Shawn," said Flower crying softly.

Flower then got up and gently kissed Shawn on his lips. She left the hospital and prayed on her way home that God would somehow grant them a miracle.

They arrived at 169th Street and entered Flower's old building. "Flower, listen honey, Mommy hasn't been to work in four days so if you think that you'll be okay all by yourself, I'll be on my way to work. I never touched your room so you can act like you never moved out and clean it up," said Mrs. Melinda laughing. "No, I'm only kidding, but please, make yourself comfortable and if you want to, you can even sleep in the bed that you and Shawn bought me for Christmas," added Mrs. Melinda.

"I'll stay with her," said Rosalyn.

"I'm also available, Flower," said Mrs. Berkowitz.

"Thank you guys, but no, you all go and catch up on your own business. I really appreciate you guys for being here for me. It's my first day out of that dag on hospital and I'd like a little bit of time to myself. So again, don't worry too much about me. I'll be fine. And thanks again everyone, Mommy, Mrs. Berkowitz, Ros. I couldn't have done it without you all," said Flower.

"Flow, let me at least help you upstairs," said Rosalyn.

"Okay."

"Alright Flower, I'll see you when I get home," said Mrs. Melinda.

"Call me if you need anything darling. Anything!" said Mrs. Berkowitz.

"I will. See ya!" said Flower walking toward the elevator.

Flower and Rosalyn rode up seven stories to reach Flower's mother's house and once Flower was safe inside, Rosalyn continued upstairs, walking one extra flight to reach her own apartment. Flower walked to her old bedroom and laid out a panty and bra set along with some old pajamas that she found in the old dresser that she left behind. She checked her mother's room to see how she redecorated after she and Shawn purchased her mom a brand new bedroom set for 1996 Christmas. Flower sat at the edge of her mother's bed and scanned the room looking for the remote control to the television. She noticed that her mom had purchased a new cordless phone so she decided to pick it up and examine it. "I wonder if her voice mail code is still the same?" she thought. After dialing a few digits into the handset, the telephone started to ring on the other end.

Ring! Ring! Ring! Ring!

"Please enter your access code," said the recording.

Subconsciously thinking, Flower began pressing numbers.

"Boop-Boop-Beep-Bop! You have one message. Boooop! Hello Mom, it's me." Flower heard her own voice and wondered when she left the message. She then heard the rest of the horrific message. "Click! Click! Listen here Player, let me hold that!" The voice Flower was hearing was very familiar. "You won't be needing these keys for a while! And while you're at it, let me get that watch, that bracelet, that chain, those rings and that bulge in your pocket! Yeah that too Homie!"

Flower went into a temporary state of shock as the incident that nearly took her life less than a week ago and left her fiancé in a coma played back into her head. The voice that spoke those creepy words belonged to none other than Raheem, Rosalyn's ex-boyfriend. He was the man who shot and robbed Shawn. The person who shot Flower was still undetermined, but wherever Raheem was, the other shooter was sure to be close by. As the minutes passed slowly, Flower regained her composure thinking only one thing, 'Payback!' Flower picked up the phone and called Rosalyn.

Flower's Bed

Ring! Ring!

"Hello," said Rosalyn.

"Aye girl, it's me," said Flower.

"Hold on Flow, let me hang up with London."

Click!

"Hello."

"Yeah Ros, I see your new man got that ass strung out. But we'll never know unless you're completely over Raheem," said Flower.

"Flow, I've been over Raheem's ass. What took the cake was when I found out that he be at The Sugar Shack Strip Bar on Hunt's Point Avenue fucking with them snow bunnies."

"Oh he done left the dark meat and graduated to fucking with them white hoes? Let me find out that you wasn't sucking that thing like you were trying to get to the center of a Blow Pop," said Flower.

"It wasn't even like that. He hooked up with some nigga named Omar that just came home from jail. Them two mothafuckas are inseparable now. I think when Raheem takes a shit, Omar wipes his ass for him, and vice versa."

"I heard that," said Flower laughing.

"But the kid Omar is on white bitches hard. Him and Raheem started having foursomes with some white girls they met at a Rave party down at the Paladium about eight months ago. His ass has had Jungle Fever ever since. I don't even speak to that fat mothafucka anymore."

"Does he ever try and contact you thinking that he's going to get some?"

"Flow, that nigga is turned all the way out. His ass stays in that club 24/7. If he's not out here on the late night selling his little rocks and stuff, he's in that damn club."

"He'll learn one day that it's not a good idea to leave us black women for dead. I promise you he'll learn his lesson," said Flower firmly. "So what's up with London? Did he give you your groove back?"

"Girl, that nigga said he don't eat pussy! That's the only thing that I hate about some of these West Indian niggas, they act like they don't eat the coochie. But London uses this stuff called Stone. You rub it on the underside of your dick and once you get it up, it ain't going back down until both of you are sore from fucking."

"Ain't that what you wanted?"

"I mean it's cool, but he's really long. I guess he was blessed with length and not width and that shit be poking my stomach sometimes."

"It's better than having a pinky sized thing to work with."

"You're right about that."

"Listen Ros, I'm going to holla at you later. I just wanted to see what you were doing."

"Nothing, I should be here until around nine o'clock tonight. That's when London gets off work and picks me up. Then we go over to his house and he reminds me over and over why they call him Yard Mon. But I'll be here for a while. Call me."

"I will."

"Bye, bye."

"Bye."

Click!

Flower dials another number.

Ring! Ring! Ring! Ring!

"Hello, the V.I.P. Club, Joey speaking."

"Hey Joe, it's me, Angel."

"Angel, we have a hundred Angels that work here," said the bartender talking over the loud music.

"Does Mt. Everchest still work there?"

"Yeah, Eve still works here. She won't be in for another two hours though. You want me to take a message?"

"Yeah."

"Forgetaboutit."

Click!

"Let me get my ass in the tub and iron my clothes," thought Flower to herself.

An hour and a half later, Flower was in a taxicab on her way to the V.I.P. Club. She arrived and was allowed in without having to pay the entrance fee because the old bouncer, Jimmy, was still the door guy. Flower walked down to the dressing room where she saw an all new cast of ladies.

"And girl, I had him cumming in less than two minutes," said Mt. Everchest talking to the different group of ladies. "Girl, is that you? Is that my Angel?" said Mt. Everchest looking past the girls. Seeing that it was her, Mt. Everchest stretched out her arms to embrace Flower.

"Hey Angel, how are you? It's been too long girl," said Mt. Everchest. "You look a little under the weather too. Is everything alright?" she said looking Flower up and down.

"I had a little accident. Nothing major. I'll be okay."

"You're still looking good. So how've you been?"

"I've been good. I'm working. I moved."

"Where? Did you move with that one dude?" said Mt. Everchest smiling.

"No, actually, I moved down south by myself. I'm going to Hampton University in Virginia."

"Wonderful. So what brings you back this way?"

"I need a favor."

"You need money? I got myself a little stash, but honey, I always got enough to share with a friend," said Mt. Everchest, digging for her money she had stashed in her cleavage.

"It's not money that I need. You see there's this guy," said Flower, placing her hand on Mt. Everchest's hand stopping her from retrieving her loot.

"Uh oh, I thought you were done with the bullshit."

"I am done, but I met this one guy and I thought he was the one. So he and I end up getting close and I find out that the son-of-a-bitch is married. Not only was he cheating on his wife with me, he also has this fetish for white women."

"So what, are you trying to hook me up?" said Mt. Everchest giving Flower a look that said, "Girl, you must be crazy."

"No Eve, I just need to place his ass in a situation where I can frame his ass. Take some pictures of something. I could use that money to pay for school. You feel me?"

"And you need E-V-E to help you pull it off?" said Mt. Everchest folding her arms.

"Sort of. You see, he won't come near me anymore because he knows what he did to me almost hit my heart. But God put something there to protect me and also helped me find out about his scheme."

"So what do you need me to do?" said Mt. Everchest, always willing to save the day.

"Let's walk upstairs to the bar," said Flower. "I'm going to need a drink for this one."

Mt. Everchest sat patiently at the bar with Flower as everything was explained in detail that needed to be done.

"So when should I be ready Flow?"

"Be ready at around eleven o'clock tomorrow evening. We'll roll out then."

"I got you ma."

"Thanks a lot Eve. I owe you one. Oh yeah, what ever happened to Cherry and Cinnamon?" asked Flower.

"Oh yeah, I didn't tell you. Cherry is a part of her church's choir and she's engaged to a brother that goes to church with her, and Cin is in John Jay studying law. She's in love with some Spanish guy that she met near her school. He's supposed to own a pool hall, a restaurant and a cab stand somewhere on Amsterdam Avenue. I hope he ain't one of those Dominican drug dealers though," she said laughing.

"Well I hope everything works out for them."

"Me too."

"See you tomorrow night."

"I won't be late." Mt. Everchest waved goodbye to Flower.

The following evening, Flower recovered the gun that she had retrieved from J.R.'s apartment over two years ago. She kept it safely hidden in between her mattresses in the bed at her mother's house. She practically forgot about it and was happy that she had experience with guns from being at the shooting range with Shawn in Scranton, Pennsylvania. Flower checked it to make sure that it was still loaded and looked for the safety button to make sure it was secure. Shawn had taught her how to handle a weapon, how to aim it, how to shoot one and how to wipe off her fingerprints although he felt she wouldn't need to. It was getting close to eleven o'clock so Flower called herself a taxicab and decided not to talk to her Lord this evening. The cab pulled up and had her at the V.I.P. Club shortly after eleven o'clock.

"Psss! Pssss!" said Mt. Everchest calling for Flower. "Over here," she whispered from an alleyway on the side of the club.

Flower spotted her friend in her sexy getup that she asked her to wear. And after all of the time that had passed, Mt. Everchest still looked good.

"Damn girl, you got me second guessing about my own damn preference. Look at you. You look gorgeous girl," said Flower.

"Thank you. This is one of my special hookups that is guaranteed to get any man open. I usually only bring it out for my King Tut. Remember him?" said Mt. Everchest fixing her clothes.

"Can't forget Mr. Anaconda," said Flower laughing along with Mt. Everchest.

"Are you ready?" asked Mt. Everchest.

"Ready when you are. Where's your car?" asked Flower.

"I brought the minivan. Just in case I run into one of my regulars. I can act like I'm with my husband."

"Eve you're crazy. Let's get going!"

The two of them rode from the V.I.P. Club to The Sugar Shack Club on Hunt's Point Avenue in twenty minutes' time.

"Go ahead Eve, do your thing," said Flower as Eve exited the vehicle and walked into The Sugar Shack Club.

Inside the club, the atmosphere was similar to the V.I.P. Club except this place was smaller and had only one large V.I.P. booth. There were three poles on the stage and the place was barely lit. Hip hop music blared through the speakers as women with a much lower class of style than those at the V.I.P. Club entertained customers of all kinds. When Mt. Everchest came across two guys, one of which fit the description of Raheem, she strutted her stuff in the small area in front of them.

"Daaamn! Who on God's earth are you?" asked Raheem excitedly.

"I'm Available, and at your service whenever you want me big boy," said Mt. Everchest with a seductive smile.

"Ayo 'O', you see big girl? Mamma got it going on!" said Raheem, mesmerized by Mt. Everchest's dance moves.

"Aye, Ms. Available, why don't you come on over here and have a seat with the man," said Omar.

Mt. Everchest walked in between Raheem and his friend making Omar scoot over. She slowly lowered herself into the seat never taking her eyes from Raheem's.

"What is a big girl like yourself doing down in this here neck of the woods?" asked Raheem.

"I'm here visiting from out of town. I was getting bored so I figured that I'd come outside and find something to do."

"So did you find out what it is that you want to do?" asked Omar.

"Not yet. The activities that I call for require more than just plain ol' me."

"Ain't nothing plain about you girl. The question is, can you handle the both of us?" asked Raheem, pointing at Omar.

"I think the question should be, can the two of you handle me?"

"Say no more. Yo 'O', pull the truck up front. We gon cruise on our way to the telly, go fill our bellies ya heard! It's party time!"

"Do you have a room?" asked Mt. Everchest licking her juicy red lips.

"Girl, we keep a room!"

"Does your room have a hot tub?" she asked, sucking on one of her fingers.

"What the hell do we need a hot tub for? I got all the hot juice right here," said Raheem pointing at his crotch.

"Well I like to get wet inside and out. Now if you boys don't have a room with a hot tub in it, we can use mine. You guys are just going to have to refund me for it."

"No problem. How much?"

"Two hundred dollars."

"Two hundred dollars? Daaaamn!" said Omar.

"Oh you thought this coochie was free?"

"Nigga just give her the damn money!" said Raheem.

Pulling out two one hundred dollar bills, Omar passed Mt. Everchest the money.

"Where to?" he asked.

"The Cross Country Inn, Co-op City. Section Two," replied Mt. Everchest.

Ten minutes later …

Omar pulled up in front of the room and the trio exited the truck. They entered the room and found candles lit all around the hot tub.

"It's on tonight!" said Raheem excitedly.

"Come here big boy," said Mt. Everchest as she walked toward Raheem.

She grabbed him by the back of his head and licked his whole face in one motion. When Omar walked up behind her she let him grab her waist as she touched his crotch area, then she said, "I want to be in control. You! Lay on the bed!" she said, talking to Omar. Omar jumped on the bed with his shirt off and Mt. Everchest walked over to him, looked him seductively in his eyes and she began tying his wrists and ankles to the bedposts. Unzippering his pants, Mt. Everchest took Omar's member into her mouth and deep throated him keeping her mouth on his penis for four seconds. She looked over at Raheem and said, "If you want some of this fat pussy, your ass better strip all the way naked boy!"

Raheem came out of his clothing like he was in a one piece, all at the same time.

"Now lay your big ass on that bed and let me taste you like you've never been tasted before!" She pulled out two pairs of handcuffs and cuffed both of his arms together at the head of the bed he was on. She then tied his legs to each post at the foot of the bed with his socks. Mt. Everchest then took Raheem into her mouth until he became erect. She then climbed on the bed as if to ride him, but stopped in mid air. "Is he loosening up those ropes? Are you coming a loose over there?" said Mt. Everchest looking over at Omar.

"No, I'm tight," said Omar, reassuring Mt. Everchest by tugging on ropes that held him secured to the bedposts.

"Damn nigga, let her tighten your ropes stupid ass. Go ahead Available, tighten them shits till his blood stop circulating for all I care. Let's just fuck already," said Raheem.

She tightened Omar's ropes extra tight assuring herself that he wouldn't get loose. And for some reason, she didn't like Omar.

"Are your legs strapped in big boy. I don't need you bucking like the horse you are when you cum inside of this white goddess."

"I'm strapped tight! Check it if you're not sure!" said Raheem.

Walking back over to Raheem and securing his leg straps, Mt. Everchest got up and said, "I'll be right back fellas." She grabbed her things and exited the room. Seeing Flower outside made her feel a whole lot better. "Do you have your camera girl?" asked Mt. Everchest.

"Like the paparazzi," said Flower.

"Go get 'em then!"

"Here ma, take my Maxima back to the V.I.P. and I'll meet you there when I'm done."

"Okay Ange, I'll see you later."

Flower waited until Mt. Everchest was out of sight before she entered the room.

"We are going to fuck the shit out of this bitch tonight homie! My dick is harder than Chinese arithmetic!" said Raheem.

"Yo that bitch is teasing us. I'm going to fuck her in the ass all night for trying to fuck with my emotions!" said Omar.

"Shut the fuck up you fucking peon!" said Flower closing the door behind her. She held J.R.'s 9 mm with both hands, the way she was taught to do at the gun range.

"Flower, what the hell is wrong with you bitch? You done went crazy or something? Untie my ass before I drop you like I dropped your stupid ass friend. Untie me hoe!" said Raheem.

Flower aimed the gun at Omar's stiff penis and let off one shot, "Boom!" blowing the top half of his penis to smithereens, leaving what was left looking like a Koolaid water fountain. Omar's screams were muffled by the television and the radio that Mt. Everchest raised the volume on before leaving.

"Yo my nuts! My fucking nuts! My nuts are gone Rah! Aaaagghh!" screamed Omar.

"Faggot. You thought I wouldn't come back for you two! Laugh now mothafucka!" said Flower.

"What the fuck is wrong with you? What are you talking about?" asked Raheem nervously.

"You and your bitch ass buddy here tried to kill me and my man last week in front of my mother's building over some fucking jewelry! Remember that punk! Huh bitch!" screamed Flower as she pointed the gun back at Omar and let of another shot, "Boom!" This one split his right kneecap.

Flower's Bed

"Aaaagghh! Stop this bitch Rah! She's going to kill me! What the fuck!" screamed Omar.

"Nigga shut the fuck up and stop crying like a little bitch! I should let your ass bleed to death," said Flower.

"Please ma, don't kill me. Listen, you know I always liked you right? I was only fucking your friend so that I could get close to you. Come on Flow, please, don't kill me. Please! Don't kill me!" said Raheem beginning to cry.

"It's over Raheem!"

"Wait! I'll get you your jewelry!" said Raheem trying anything to save his life.

"Fuck that jewelry, and fuck you too!" said Flower aiming the gun at different parts of Raheem's body as she spoke to herself in her head. "That watch!" She shot him in his left arm. "Boom!" "That bracelet!" She shot him in his right arm. "Boom!" "Those rings!" She shot him twice in the chest. "Boom, boom!" "That chain!" She shot him in the neck. "Boom" "And that bulge in your pocket! Yeah that too homie!" thought Flower as she raised the gun a little bit higher and delivered a final shot to his forehead ending his short life. "Booom!" She looked over at Omar who tried to close his eyes and play dead. She aimed the gun at his chest and said, "This is for not killing me!" She then emptied six more shells into Omar's chest killing him too. "Boom! Boom! Boom! Boom! Boom! Boom!" She kept two bullets in the gun in case she bumped into a problem on the way out. Reaching into her waistband, Flower pulled out two black roses and laid one on each of the blood-stained bodies. She walked to the window, peeked out, saw that the coast was clear and softly said, "That's what happens when you punish a bitch and don't kill her." Then she left the hotel without a trace.

CHAPTER TWENTY-THREE

Six Months Later ...

With all the major news happening around the city, the incident with Raheem and Omar was reported in a low budget local newspaper called The Bronx Times and was eventually forgotten about. It was reported that Raheem and Omar were last seen near a Hunts Point area strip bar with a six-foot white male dressed as a woman. It was also reported that the crime could've been a cover up for a drug deal gone bad because a subsequent search of both their articles of clothing turned up a recovery of cocaine and a 25. caliber semi-automatic handgun. When Raheem's jeep was recovered after it was allegedly stolen and stripped by a guy in the neighborhood named Kneecaps, the police dog at the impound yard found a hidden compartment that contained a little less than two ounces of raw heroine. The case was eventually overlooked though police still have an APB out on a lone white male, six feet, 180 pounds, dressed in drag. The police noted that anyone with information, call their Crime Stoppers hotline at 1-800-577-TIPZ.

Six months had gone by and Shawn's right shoulder had twitched on three occasions. The doctors estimated progress would occur every two months. Flower kept vigil at his bedside everyday during visiting hours hoping that one day he'd wake up. She was currently staying at home with her mother while occasionally driving out to Pennsylvania to deal with the tenants of their apartment buildings. Exactly six months to the date of the shooting, Flower sat next to Shawn holding his hand and having her usual conversation.

"Hey Shawn, how's it going? I still miss you. My mom and Ros say hello and Sarah says whenever you feel like getting up, just go right ahead and do it. Shawn, when are you going to come back to me? This is so frustrating! You're here, but then again you're not. It's like you're in jail or something and won't accept my visits. It's like I write you letters and you never write me back. At least if you were in jail you could hug and kiss me back and send me sweet letters and encouraging cards. I don't know what to wish sometimes. At times I wonder if you're in any kind of pain and whether or not we should pull the plug on you. But I'm not the one to determine if you live of die, God is. So while He's the controller and all knowing, let's leave our fate up to him. Rosalyn says I'm crazy, Sarah says I'm obsessed. My mom says I need a break, but I say I need you and you need me. Give me a sign Shawn that you're still here with me. Why won't you wake up? You're still breathing. Aaaww." said Flower leaning her head into her chest. Crying softly, Flower felt Shawn's hand tighten up around her own. She popped her head up and looked at his eyes twitching. His head began to slowly jerk back and forth side to side and his legs started to jump.

"Oh my God! Oh my God! Nurse! Nurse! Somebody!" screamed Flower as a floor nurse ran into the coma unit.

"What's the matter Miss?" asked the nurse.

"Look, he's moving!" said Flower.

The nurse couldn't believe her eyes. "Oh my God, he is moving."

She ran over to the door and called for some assistance. As more nurses and doctors filled the room, Flower was told to wait in the waiting area.

Eight hours had gone by and Flower was falling in and out of sleep.

"Ms. Abrams! Ms. Abrams!" called a nurse.

"Yes ma'am," said Flower.

"Would you come this way please?"

The nurse brought Flower over to Shawn's room where he was moved to. The two of them caught eye contact through a glass window that lined the wall in his private room.

"He knows it's you. All he kept asking for was Angel. I guess God appointed him an angel while he slept. That happens you know. People say they've had angels with them in their comas telling them to hold on. And the angel is sometimes in the form of a loved one," said the nurse.

"Can I go in?" asked Flower.

"Sure, go right ahead."

"Shawn, oh my God. I love you! I love you! Mmtwa! Mmtwa!" said Flower kissing him.

"Be careful ma'am," said the nurse.

"Whatever. Hi honey. Can you hear me?" asked Flower.

Shawn nodded.

As the days went on, Shawn progressed more and more. After three days, he actually began to speak. He was eventually released after three months, but had to attend therapy sessions everyday until he was able to function on his own. The doctors told Flower that Shawn would make a full recovery, but it would take some time. Flower didn't care, as long as they were together, they had all the time in the world.

One day at their home in Reading, Pennsylvania, Shawn told Flower about a dream he thought he kept having while in his coma.

"Honey," said Shawn.

"Yes Shawn," said Flower.

Flower's Bed

"You know, when I was in that coma, I knew I was in a bed. Somebody's bed. In the dream, I would toss and turn and I'd wake up and see this silhouette lying next to me. But when I'd reach for it, it was too far for me to touch so I would lay there and wonder, 'Whose bed am I in?' Then I guess right before I began to regain consciousness, the silhouette began to take shape. I got nervous at first, but then I relaxed when I realized the shape of the silhouette belonged to the most important person in the world to me. It was you Flower. That silhouette was you all along. And only then was I able to sleep comfortably in my dream because I knew where I was. I was in Flower's Bed!"

FINAL WORD

To every woman in the struggle and every woman that's not in the struggle. To every lady in the struggle and every lady that's not in the struggle. To every girl, chick, grandmother, daughter, aunt, sweetheart, wifey , Boo, girlfriend, homegirl, mistress, shorty, princess, queen, neice, stepdaughter. To every one of you on the face of this earth, you are Royalty, and you should be treated as such...

ACKNOWLEDGEMENTS!

Edenwald, The Bx, we did it again, Holla at your boy! I'd like to give crazy shout outs to everybody, my moms, my sisters, my aunts, my cousins, my wife, my kids. it's going down ya heard! And to all of my peoples in the belly and on the bricks, I got love, homies. One!

Flower's Bed

by Antoine "Inch" Thomas

ORDER FORM

Copy this order form for a friend!

ISBN# 0-9745075-0-4

Please Provide Us With Your Mailing Information:

Who is placing the order?

Your Name: ______________________________

Your Address: ______________________________

Suite/ Apartment #______________________________

City: ____________________ State: ______________

Zip Code: ____________

How many copies would you like? _____

Mailing Options:

PRIORITY POSTAGE (4-6 DAYS US MAIL): Add $4.95

(All Postal rates are subject to change.)

After June 2004, Please check with your local Post Office for rates and schedules.

Where would you like the book shipped?

Name:______________________________

Address:______________________________

____

City:____________________State:__________ Zip:__________

Send Institutional Checks Or Money Order.

AMIAYA ENTERTAINMENT
P.O. BOX 1275
NEW YORK, NY 10159
212-946-6565

WWW.FLOWERSBED.COM

Federal & State prisoners, please include your Inmate Registration Number

Fan Mail Page

If you have any further questions, comments or concerns, kindly address your inquiries in care of:

Antoine "Inch" Thomas
at

AMIAYA ENTERTAINMENT
P.O. BOX 1275
NEW YORK, NY 10159

by Antoine "Inch" Thomas

COMING SOON 2004...

NO REGRETS

Also by

Antoine "Inch" Thomas

(It's what the hood 's been waitin' for)

WWW.FLOWERSBED.COM